EARTH AGAINST THE
UNKNOWN ...

'What do you think the Deeans are up to?'
'Another ship has come,' said Nicer. 'Their
third in a hundred years.'
'Do we care?'
'Not basically.'
'Suppose this time it's conquest?'

Also by A. E. Van Vogt in Sphere Books

The Secret Galactics

A. E. VAN VOGT

SPHERE BOOKS LIMITED
30/32 Gray's Inn Road, London WC1X 8JL

First published in Great Britain by Sidgwick & Jackson
Ltd 1975
Copyright © 1974 by A. E. Van Vogt
Published by Sphere Books Ltd 1977
Reprinted 1979

Set in Photon Times

Printed in Great Britain by
C. Nicholls & Company Ltd
The Phillips Park Press, Manchester

CONTENTS

From: *Galactoid–Embrid Institute, Deea Branch*
To: *All Invasion Force Personnel*
Subject: *Human Women*

URGENT

It should be noted that there is a developing interest in the above-named subject. More of the galactic groups, which have utilized our services from time to time, have decided to expand their earth commitment, and our own attempted conquest is about to begin.

Members already operating on that planet long ago secretly brought to earth embryos of their several races – male embryos only – and, utilizing the special Luind technique, transformed the embryos so that, when they grew up, they looked like, and in fact were in all important essentials, human men.

Like the rest of the men on earth, they then had the problem of dealing with human females.

Earth – for those who do not know it – is the third planet of Sol, a sun 36,000 light-years from the central galactic axis of the Milky Way galaxy. The sun is a yellow G-type and can be seen on enlarged stellar maps as a tiny point of light almost exactly on the edge of one plane of this particular wheel-shaped spiral galaxy.

It is agreed by all: women of earth have to be experienced to be believed. In the entire universe there seems to be no female quite so complex and unpredictable. Human women have been a mystery to their men from prehistoric times.

It is well to note that earth women evolved in the particularly severe environment provided for them by their men. Outwardly, when first viewed, human males seem to be reasonable, kind, goodnatured types with many worthwhile qualities. But in fact the women have found a percentage of them to be prejudiced, negating, restricting, determined to maintain total control.

These male characteristics and other qualities of the three principal types of earth males – Real Men, Sex Beggars and Inverts – are one aspect of the problem that must be confronted in the conquest of this planet. The other aspect is of course the women. Here we have to deal with the four uncriticisable attitudes that we find in women. Also we have women in the shatter condition (many complex responses here), women in racial frames, women getting even, yelling women, women as workers, women Being Beautiful, women operating in a Secondary Philosophy, women who are 200% for their men, women who keep one well-shod foot out the door (so to speak) . . . women, women, women –

Since at first we invaders did not understand all this, it is not surprising that women of earth in these early stages of the invasion have been the principal cause of our failure so far in unexpected and even dismaying ways.

Transmission begins . . .

Chapter One

MAN OF NOTHING

Shortly after midnight –

In a manner of speaking, the phone rang inside Carl.

Actually, what happened was the phone in the laboratory jingled. Instantly, a relay activated, connecting with a radio-TV transmitter – which triggered a 'receiver' inside the six-wheeled vehicle that contained Carl. He thereupon 'heard' the ringing with his auditory exteroceptors.

Carl was a mobile structure. At the top of him was a plastic, transparent dome, and inside this was a curved, mirror-like container with clear liquid half-filling it. Partly submerged in the liquid, anchored in by almost invisible plastic, Carl's pink and grey brain was visible. Different coloured tubes were attached to the brain from below.

The lower section of Carl was the computer and other equipment through which Carl's disembodied brain operated the exteroceptor motors and his electronic eyes, ears, and voice box.

The transparent dome with its brain, and the machinery below it, rested solidly on a six-wheeled truck.

As his brain leaped out of sleep, Carl closed a relay which switched on the phone in the laboratory exactly as if somebody had picked up the receiver.

From inside his brain, utilizing the elements of his voice from the years-ago recorded tapes, he controlled the mechanism by which an electronic voice box spoke the words. He said, 'Hello. This is Carl.'

'Carl, it *is* you!' said a woman's intense voice.

He thought: – Good God! . . . *her*!

The thoughts which at that moment did a skitter movement through his mind included an astonished realization: he hadn't considered her among his suspects.

Almost all the others were there: the women at Non-

9

Pareil; the shady mistresses from the nightclubs mostly, whose beauty and talent had attracted him; the promoted call girls (promoted to be on salary as secretaries), and a number of desirable female bodies that fitted no particular psychologic category. Yet he had mentally and with suspicion taken note of each and every one; and in greater or lesser degree they – or rather somebody in their background – were all possibilities in his gallery of people who might have murdered him a year ago.

Yes, murdered him.

But not Silver.

And, really, the group behind her was the most likely suspect.

As the jumble of astonishment and memory completed, Carl realized she was speaking again, almost breathlessly, 'I won't ask you where you've been all these months. I'm so glad to hear your voice again, and to realize you're all right. You can tell me the details later. Now, listen! Go at once to –'

She gave him an address. As in the past, it was one of the swank residential districts. 'There's a man there, dead. The alienoids got him. But they couldn't find what they wanted: a letter. Carl, you must go to the body and read that letter. It's incredibly important in some way that I haven't been able to find out. I'll phone you there. Goodbye.'

'Hey, wait – what? –'

The click of the receiver being replaced came with finality through his own receptors.

As he disconnected his own equipment for the phone, Carl was briefly caught up in images of his past association with the woman, Silver. But the emotion that kept coming was that her call, now, required an unexpectedly swift decision from him.

It was a new thought for a man who, until recently, had been totally – but *totally* – immobile for over a year.

From *him*. A decison.

Man of nothing. Contacted now by a woman to whom he had once (during a period) made love. The most neuter male, now, ever, anywhere. Possessed of a bodiless brain, and without a skin to receive touch, or a hand to feel with. Yet, somehow, still a male in his thinking and his attitude.

10

Gender, it would seem, is in the brain, not in the genitals. Behind him was a babyhood and a childhood of being an exceptionally honest, puzzled, curious boy. But with the teens came the change. After a faltering, naive beginning, he had been one of the fellows in *his* high school who really made it with the girls. And of course at college – wow! Money, good brains, hard study, and girls, girls, girls.

Yet here he was, twenty years later, like this –

Silver's call was, nevertheless, it seemed to Carl, a remarkable opportunity.

But – he'd have to tell somebody where he was going . . . if he went.

Who?

Tell who?

He tried, first, Dr. MacKerrie's cottage at the rear of the laboratory grounds. MacKerrie was the surgeon who had performed the delicate operation that, a year before, had transplanted Carl's brain from his dying body to a machine which, until recently, had been immobile and restricted in other ways.

After two rings, there was the familiar sound – familiar to Carl – of a recorder turning on. The voice of MacKerrie said, 'The rest of this week, beginning August 23, I can be reached daytimes at the Brain Foundation, and evenings at –' He gave a number.

Carl did a mental calculation on how long it would take MacKerrie to get out of bed and drive over to the Hazzard Laboratories . . . Too long.

With that, he reluctantly accepted that, since his one remaining option to call his wife (which, of course, would be madness; Marie would never understand), he would have to leave a tape account for MacKerrie. And that would be his sole protective action.

Chapter Two

BEYOND THE BARRIERS

The night streets were brightly lighted. Traffic was still quite heavy. Carl drove easily. In the seat behind what appeared to be the steering wheel, the human dummy sitting there went through a series of motions, which any person casually glancing toward him would take to be those of a real human male in a moving vehicle.

The movements of the puppet were activated by gears fitted into its works, and driven by a toy-sized motor with a separate connection to the compressed air tank.

The continuing . . . neutral . . . perfection of the journey made it possible for him to become aware that he was disturbed.

Just thinking about Marie's possible reaction to what he was doing had – he realized – upset him. Marie believed, with a woman's perversity, that he would never have got himself killed in the first place if he had used good sense. She seemed to be unaware that women also (for God's sake) were problems.

He was waiting for a red light to change, as he had that thought. A dozen people at that moment were charging across the busy intersection. Carl actually suppressed an impulse to call to them: 'You, there, listen. There *is* a man's side to the man-woman thing. It isn't all a case of guilty male and innocent, injured female.

'Listen – when I was in my teens –'

He had been fourteen, when, after discovering the delights of sex by way of Onanism, a simple, logical thought had struck him. Accordingly, he had approached a particularly attractive young high school miss, pointed out that between them they possessed all the equipment necessary for thorough co-exploration of the whole sex bit, and proposed that they begin forthwith during every possible private moment.

The young lady's outraged reaction caught him by surprise. She began by slapping his face. Then she told him what an awful person he was.

After he had recovered, and it still seemed like a sensible idea, he subsequently made the same proposition to four other young ladies – and then gave up, baffled. A couple of months later, a youthful male acquaintance, in a boastful mood, mentioned that he was having an affair with the first girl.

'I gave her the usual line,' he said. 'About how I'd fallen for her, and wanted to marry her, and how life had meaning for me now that I'd discovered she was in the world.'

'You mean June?' said Carl, interested.

'Yeah, June.'

'She fell for that?'

'Yep. Just like they all do. Or some variation – you know, fit the honey to the particular bee.'

Carl was bemused, recalling how he had pointed out to June something that he had already decided was true: that in fact life had *no* meaning, that their relationship probably wouldn't last very long in a changing world, and that of course at the moment he had no plans for marriage. So – it had seemed logical to him – let's have fun while we can.

– Good God! he had thought, as the inanity of his approach burst upon him.

'You mean,' he said to his informant, 'your system works. Girls are like *that*.'

'Never failed me yet,' said the boastful one.

From that moment of insight, Carl surged forward into the female universe with total power.

The memory stirred him anew to a sense of the injustice of what Marie would think . . . She fell for my line just like the others did – There was only one puzzling aspect to the relationship . . . Why did I marry *her*? –

The biggest lemon this side of Florida. And not only had he married her, but he'd stayed with her after she turned sour.

Fourteen years, for heaven's sake –

He was about to attempt one more baffling analysis of that improbable act . . . when he spotted the house he was looking for.

Instantly, Marie, sex, and his teen conquests faded from his mind.

He could do things like that: concentrate.

He began by making his usual preliminary survey. He drove around the block. And happily discovered there was a back alley.

Into this he guided the panel truck. The best place to park – it turned out – was beside the fence of the house that was his destination. It indented slightly, giving him more room for the car. It was from the comparative darkness of his location beside the fence that Carl studied his situation.

And now he was in a dilemma. Until his 'death' a year before, he had entered such houses as this with the ease of a powerful man in his early forties. Like a cat burglar, he vaulted fences, climbed into windows, scrambled over roofs.

But now – how to manipulate the six-wheeled unit that was the cumbersome physical body, all that remained, of a once agile man? Manipulate it through gates, through locked doors, up stairways.

It seemed impossible. Yet he knew that compressed air power, and the flexibility of the wheel system, made possible actions and movements that would otherwise be out of the question.

Without further hesitation, Carl unlocked the rear opening of the truck and rolled down onto the rough pavement of the alleyway. There was a back gate. As he anticipated, it was padlocked from inside. But his hands reached with their crane-like extensors; reached over and reached down.

For an instant, then, Carl peered at the barrier through a tiny TV camera set into a little hole in one steel arm. What he saw was a padlock . . . With a single, sharp movement of the steel 'hands' he snapped the lock in two.

The sound of the metal breaking was almost inaudible.

But the miniscule click as it cracked apart had an effect on him. Out of proportion excitement . . . I'm enjoying this.

That was something women never understood, he thought. For a Real Man – Carl hesitated over the appellation as applied to himself; he was remembering the particular female who had in an over-sweet voice labelled him with the term one day; it was that sharp-minded Craig

14

woman. Yet even then he was objective enough in his thinking to notice that it had a certain applicability . . . for a Real Man, danger actually was a stimulant. Women – those scaredy cats! – would never know how exhilarating it was to be in a battle, cool, observant, alert, prepared to do violence and face any consequences. Only males, it seemed to Carl, who are able to be like that, could ever call themselves *men* –

The intense feeling continued, needing no body of flesh and blood to experience it. It seemed to derive in part from his awareness that he could do things in his present state that no human being could match.

It was, literally, a sense of power. Realization came that the motor centres in his brain were probably free of the restraint normal to the average ageing human. In that condition was pleasure in movement. In doing. In – danger.

Unhesitating now, impelled by those energetic impulses, Carl pushed the gate open. Silently, he rolled through. Quickly, he closed the gate behind him, and, without pause, headed for the rear of the house.

The back door was made of wood, with an ordinary Yale lock. Carl burned a curving slit out of the wood all the way around the lock, pushed the door open, and rolled up the three steps and into the house. It was easier than he had expected. What made it possible was the forcing power of compressed air and the flexibility inherent in a six-wheeled vehicle, wherein each wheel could be manipulated separately.

He was relieved. Not quite the smoothness of human muscles, but the steel-and-motor strength was a powerful plus factor.

He found the dead body in the library.

Chapter Three

'THE SHIP IS COMING!'

Carl forced himself to take his usual precautions. He listened. Heard nothing. Well . ... street sounds, passing cars, distant night movements of the city. But nothing in the house.

Were there people asleep upstairs? – Or was this one of those lucky times when the murdered man and his observer had a large two-storey mansion to themselves under the protecting mantle of a night that was still in its early stage of darkness? It would be unwise to believe that the situation was that secure for him.

The implication of danger did not seem to disturb him. And, in fact, at that precise moment he 'felt' the letter; and his awareness of his surroundings dimmed. For him, feeling meant that electronic sensors scanned what the finger extensions were touching, consulted a computer memory, and identified what was being felt as paper.

He drew the letter out of its envelope carefully – it required both hand extensors and several finger extensions in an intricate, balanced manoeuvre – one important precaution had to be that he did not tear the damn thing into little pieces. So easy to do with all that incredibly strong motor-driven metal.

Yet, presently, he had the letter unfolded, and had read it. He folded it, puzzled. The message in the letter was brief. It was simply a mimeographed – or some such copy system – announcement of the imminent arrival of a ship named *Takeover*, and ordered all of the 'true people' to stand by for Operation C.

Carl thought, baffled: Takeover of *what*?

But it didn't seem important. So what was all the fuss about? . . . As he considered possibilities of meaning, he awkwardly went through the innumerable movements of metal hands and fumbling fingers slipping it back into its envelope, and then laboriously putting the envelope back into the secret pocket in the lower inside lining of a coat – all without disturbing the still body more than he absolutely had to.

He was totally in the clear, actually rolling away – backing – from the body, when the phone rang once.

Her signal.

There would be a pause, he knew; and, abruptly, he felt the old thrill. Strange to have so rich a recollection of a former feeling. But he had already discovered that with his brain alone he was capable of all the emotions.

Now, of this one! ... While he mentally timed the delay that she normally – in the past – had allowed him, he did again what he had in the days when he was still a living body: except instead of walking he rolled over to the phone on his rubber wheels. And waited there. But he was not inactive. One set of hand extensors swiftly removed the receiver. Another set pressed down the phone buttons thus making sure that the instrument, in effect, was still in its quiescent state and as if the receiver was in position.

The receiver itself he inserted into a little door of himself and laid it face down on the electronic receiving equipment that was there.

Thus, when the phone rang again, he was ready. To begin with, at the very first sound – the barest start of the ring – he removed his 'hand' from the phone buttons. The sound ceased.

... Experience had established that people did not usually awaken from a deep sleep on a single ring. So, if there *was* someone upstairs asleep, then the possible precautions were taken.

Of course, if the person up there was already awake – well, that had happened several times, also. In the past, the answer to that had been to act swiftly.

Carl acted; had his voice box utter the word, 'Yes?' in a soft, questioning tone. The voice box was already interconnected with the equipment on which the receiver lay. So the word went out over the line.

'Carl –' Her voice came through another relay to his own

17

hearing complex; and, as before, he felt the old thrill of excitement. In the past, the thrill had been partly due to the stimulation of the thought of the sex they would have later.

Now, as he remembered the true state of his being, the high excitement faded. He answered in a low voice, 'Yes.'

Meaning – yes, it's I.

'What have you found? What's in the letter?'

He summarized it for her in a low voice. Before he could finish, she said, 'Oh, my God – does it give a date?'

'No. But, I gather you know what this ship is. Tell me.'

'Later. Right now – listen! Carl, someone is coming. Not just one; several. They're furious at the murderer for failing to find the letter. So get out of there, fast.'

'Have you called the police?'

'No, I just got the picture as I started to dial. They're awfully close, Carl. Hurry!'

'Will you call the police?'

'Yes, of course. But, now, quick!'

There was a click.

Hastily, Carl replaced his own receiver. And he was hurriedly turning actually rather noisily, for rubber wheels are not silent even in a relatively slow movement – when he heard another sharper sound.

It was the sound of a car door slamming out in the street.

Here already? Carl expected to experience a tiny chill of fear. Instead . . . stimulation came. A kind of joy. Things were happening, and he was glad.

He did the best he could with the time that remained. There was an alcove at one end of the room, which led to an open door. Into this alcove and through that door, the compressed air power drove his six-wheeled body. In the darkness beyond the door, he flashed on a dim light – and saw with relief that it was a machine room of some kind. A refrigerator, a mobile grill.

There was an empty space alongside the wall that ran at right angles to the open door. Carl spun his vehicle around in a single manoeuvre that placed him where his 'eyes' could see a good portion of the alcove just beyond, and a small view of the study room on the other side of the alcove.

She'd said they were close; so he could only hope that

18

they were also bold, or knew this house. Hope, in short, that they did not find his car sitting in the back alley. The machine was, of course, electrically locked, and would not be easy to break into – but still, it would be better not to have to defend it from such an unpleasant possibility.

Carl kept telling himself: – There's no reason why such people shouldn't use the front door.

As he had that thought, he heard sounds: A door opening, voices. Nothing quiet, here ... They were voluble like visitors arriving in broad daylight, and being very energetic about it. And it *was* through the front door. They *were* being bold. Evidently, they had reason to believe that the rest of the house was unoccupied on this murder night.

Carl acted quickly. He had television and radio contact with his car. He started the motor – by remote radio control. A television camera – the same one he used when he was in the car – watched the back alley road for him. And although he had a feeling of a difference between being in the car and operating at this distance, he realized that the feeling was largely a product of his knowing where he was.

The actual driving was no more difficult than when he was inside the panel compartment. The dummy figure at the wheel went through the same motions. The little truck itself drove straight along the alleyway to the first street, made a sharp right turn, and then drove two blocks – not because he wanted it that far away, but because that was the distance of the first parking space.

While the car moved, time passed. During that time, people came into the room where the dead body lay. Carl, intent on driving his panel truck, was vaguely aware that the number of them was ... over a dozen. During those first minutes after the first one came into view, they stood around and talked to those near them.

They were quite open. Voices were normal. It was almost as if he was the driver of a car who, while concentrating on the road ahead, could nevertheless overhear what his passengers were discussing. Except that at times there were several conversations proceeding simultaneously, and so it was not always possible to follow all of them.

The first thing Carl heard was so ordinary that at a party

he wouldn't have stayed after the first two words. But of course there he was, so to speak, in the car. And he had to listen all the way from the nothing beginning to the nothing end.

'How's Margaret?' said a man to his neighbour.

'Mad at me for going out tonight.'

'Thinks you ought to stay at home more with her and the kids?'

'Yep.'

'So does Susan feel that way about me.'

The next bit of conversation was more cryptic:

'What do you think the Luinds and the Sleeles will do when they find out about the ship?'

'Paul has already phoned Metnov. He had no particular reaction.'

'Okay, that takes care of the vicious one. What about the two sets of good guys?'

'Metnov is going to talk to the Luind leader through an aide. And of course the remaining three groups, good, bad, and indifferent, respectively, have no power, really. So the attitude is: tell them as a courtesy at the last minute. But to hell with them.'

'Hmm.' Pause. 'How's your wife?'

'Difficult, as always. She thinks I associate with the wrong people.'

The two men both laughed wryly.

For a while after that, only scattered sentences came through the confusion of voices:

'– Dorothy will be waiting up for me, so I wish Paul would hurry . . .'

'A woman is like a –' Last words missing.

'– I tell you she's so beautiful and sexy . . .' And the rest of *that* sentence was lost in somebody else's words . . .

Finally, there was one more audible interchange:

'What will we Deeans gain from this takeover?'

'More control over the women.'

Grim laughter.

Just about that time Carl completed the action of parking his car against the distant kerb. The moment he did so, it turned out, coincided with the sound of the front door opening once more. Moments after that, a large man walked into Carl's line of vision and stopped.

He was grey-haired and grey-eyed, and looked about fifty years of age. His lips were drawn together into a tight, almost angry smile. He seemed a little over-weight, but his body was otherwise solid in appearance; and there was about him, and it, a commanding air.

His face also seemed a little on the fleshy side. But it was a strong, determined face. It was the determination – it seemed to Carl – not of a mentally sick man, but of someone who believed in a truth of some kind. He had a consciousness of his own.

That consciousness, whatever it was, marked him as a dangerous man. Oddly, the question about such a man was not so much, what was his consciousness? Obviously, that could be any of a dozen ideas, nonsensical and otherwise. He could be a product of a particular brainwashing. It might even be interesting for about a quarter of a minute to listen to what he believed. But Carl, who had had his own certainties that he had lived with and by for better or worse, had long ago come to the awareness that it didn't really matter what a man thought. The question always was: what did it *drive* him to do?

This man walked forward. And he now did something which all those who had come before him had not seen fit to do. He looked around. He came to the centre of the room; and, standing there, he turned slowly full circle. During that turn, his gaze darted everywhere. When his eyes came to the alcove where Carl sat in full view, they paused. For many seconds he stood there with an appraising expression. Yet, presently, his eyes turned away.

He completed his full circle scan of the room and what was in it and adjoining. And then, in a deliberate way, he walked over to the dead body. Then he said, 'William, come over here.'

A slender, thin-faced young man, who had been standing off by himself, shuffled forward until he also stood above the murdered man. He was a sallow-complexioned individual in his middle twenties. He stood there uneasily.

The big man glanced around at the other persons in the

21

room, all men. 'We're going to have a lesson here, all of us, is my belief. That lesson is the reason why you are here.' He turned to the young man. 'All right, William, search him.'

'B-but I already did – before, when I killed him,' protested William. 'And the letter wasn't there.'

As he spoke, he made a gesture with his body and head. It was an impatient movement. His abundant yellow-brown hair, which lay on his head in essentially uncombed masses, jerked to one side, and immediately took up a different, equally unprepossessing configuration. His whole manner telegraphed a kind of rebellion against what was happening.

The big man said coldly, 'Here is a dead man. When he was still alive a few hours ago, I saw him place a letter in an inside pocket of his coat. He told me at that time that he was going to do two things. First, show the letter to an important government group over which we have no influence. And then, second, bring government agents here and give them a conducted tour of the machinery downstairs. If you'll think about it, you'll realize that the only danger to us is if we're taken into custody before the ship can help us.'

He continued grimly, 'After a threat like that, there was no turning back. And so, when he and I emerged from the restaurant where he had defied me, I signalled to William. Whereupon, William followed him home, and killed him. When William phoned me, he said he was unable to find the letter. All this was within the space of half an hour, and less than two hours ago.'

The man paused. Once more, his gaze swept the faces of the silent audience. Then: 'I would guess that there is nothing in the letter itself that would be significant to the authorities. But that machinery could be another matter. And – listen – we have had a lot of slipshod work recently, and bad re-actions. There's a hesitation in people. Every person present here tonight has been overheard making some kind of luke-warm statement about what is about to happen here on earth. There's a distinct lack of dedication. I want to show you what happens when an individual begins to be concerned about himself and loses sight of the larger goal.'

The big man glanced at William. 'Find the letter,' he commanded.

The young man knelt reluctantly. 'You could've had somebody plant it on him,' he mumbled. 'How would I know?'

The leader's gaze swept out over the audience; settled on another person. 'Henry, where was I the last two hours?'

'You were with me and Jim.'

'And did I leave your presence, and make any phone calls?'

'No.' Henry seemed vaguely unhappy. He was a tall, slender man in his late thirties; and he now felt motivated to make an additional comment. 'As most of you know,' he continued, 'I'm not hot on this takeover. And I shudder to think what my wife's reaction will be if she ever finds out that I'm involved – She thinks this is some kind of high-level Rotary club I belong to. And that it's good business for me to know a banker like Paul. But, of course –' with a curt laugh '– I never intended like our late lamented to betray our group –'

He stopped.

Nearly everyone present had made a sound. Sort of a sigh. For William was straightening, and clutched in his fingers was the letter.

'I coulda sworn –' he muttered.

'Open it,' commanded the big man, 'and read it.'

And, of course, as the watching Carl knew only too well, it was indeed the letter that William had been sent to obtain. As the words that were in it came hesitantly from the young man's lips, Carl saw the leader back slowly off to one side, and put his right hand in his coat pocket. The big man stood there, his eyes narrowed, his lips curled. Suddenly, he drew his hand out of his pocket, and there was a metallic glint in it. And then a flash of brightness.

On the floor, the kneeling figure of William . . . stiffened.

For several seconds, the silence in that room was total. Everybody stood as if frozen. Finally –

One man drew a deep, noisy breath. And, from a far corner, a small, dark, chunky man said, 'Was that really necessary?'

Another man, a fleshy-faced individual of about forty, said, 'For Christ's sake, Paul, you know damn well why

23

William didn't find the letter. The hot little blonde he's dating was probably on his mind while he was searching.'

'The time,' said Paul in that deliberate tone, 'has come to stop thinking all the time about hot blondes.'

'Look who's talking,' said a third man, with a sneer. 'The guy with the hottest blonde of them all, who just about drives him out of his mind.'

'I never let a woman interfere,' said Paul, and his voice was even-tempered, even-toned.

'That's a bunch of bushwa, and you know it,' said the same sneering voice. 'And don't try to pull that Zis on me. I'll beat you to the draw.'

Henry said mildly to the challenger, a brown-haired, sturdy man in his early thirties, 'Darrell, slow down.'

'That was a dirty, low-down murder. He wants to show us how tough he is.'

'You mean,' said Henry, 'you're not going to go along with this takeover?'

'I don't want any foolishness from Mr. Big Shot here, that's all.'

Paul stood silent while the dialogue darted past him. Now, he stirred. 'Henry – Darrell – all of you,' he said, 'get in line. The ship is coming. Understand. It's not me you're going to be dealing with. It's the ship. It's computer-controlled, remorselessly programmed. It will tolerate no weakness in anyone, not in me, not in you. It will accept no excuses. It doesn't care how much you love your wife and children. Prepare yourself, gentlemen, for total dedication – or death. There will be no exceptions.'

With that he walked over to William. Bent down. Eased the letter from under the finger. And straightened. As he slipped the letter into his own breast pocket, once more his gaze came up – and rested on Carl.

'What's that?' he said in an irritated voice. 'I don't recall seeing that on my previous visits.'

Having spoken, he walked toward Carl in that even-paced stride.

During the swift seconds that followed, several possibilities for action flashed through Carl's brain.

But he decided to do nothing. To remain where he was.

Wait – he told himself . . . Yet it would be ridiculous – and deadly – to be found out on this initial attempt to discover who his enemies were.

As Carl had these thoughts, the big man came all the way into the alcove, and stood, frowning, only a few feet from the six-wheeled monster. He shook his head baffled. Without glancing around, he said, 'You engineers back there – got any idea what this is?'

Without pausing for a reply, he stepped forward and gingerly placed his palm on the smooth, hard metal that covered the plastic dome, inside which was Carl's brain. 'Cool,' he said. He added, 'Whatever it is, it's not switched on.'

Another man had come forward into the alcove. He knelt down and peered at Carl's underside. 'It's all sealed in,' he announced. He climbed to his feet, and said in a low voice, 'Listen, Paul. Our job should be to get rid of these dead bodies, and get out of here. Let's not waste –'

At that instant, the phone rang; and the speaker paused.

All over the room, except for the ringing phone, there was silence.

Finally, the big man whispered, 'It will stop ringing in a moment. Let's wait.'

It rang twenty times. Then it rang twenty more times. Then: 'Henry,' said the big man, 'answer it.'

Carl correctly remembered Henry as the tall man, and it was indeed he who stepped forward and picked up the receiver, and said, 'Hello.' After a moment, a strange expression came into his face, and the colour drained from his cheeks. He turned slowly, placed his palm over the mouthpiece, and said in a shaken voice, 'It's the police. They say the house is surrounded. They want us to come out one by one.'

Carl thought: 'Oh, good girl, Silver. She did it.'

He saw another, larger possibility: that his own personal problem with these people would be solved with their arrest.

He was instantly exultant. In one night, everything. What fantastic good fortune.

In the large room, the men started to mill around. It was a phenomenon of emotion, Carl noted; and it was fascinating to watch.

25

Every single person, except the big man and Henry – who was at the phone – moved swiftly from where he had been. It was a reaction only. Nobody went anywhere, really. And after a few moments, they were frozen again.

The big man, who had watched the spectacle with an expression of contempt, now said to Henry, 'Tell the police we'll come out as directed.' He waited while the tall man did so. Then: 'Hang up.'

Henry put the receiver down on its cradle; and Paul continued, 'Don't you realize, all of you –' his tone was seething – 'that this doesn't mean anything. Our story will be simply that we were invited here – and found the bodies.'

He addressed Henry again, 'Phone Gilbert and have him get over to the police station. I want him there when we arrive.'

The thin man hastily consulted a little notebook and then dialled a number. Henry listened for several seconds, then looked up, shaking his head, 'He's not home.'

Paul's face had turned brick red. But still he maintained that dead-level voice, 'Okay, call Silver. Tell her the situation. Tell her to contact either Gilbert or one of the others like him, as quickly as possible. She'll understand.'

Henry dialled with quick nervous movements. But after a minute he reported reluctantly. 'No answer, sir.'

Carl, who had been watching again, and listening with a return of his detachment, felt a second surge of elation as the name, Silver, was spoken. He was awed. In a single visit, not only was he instrumental in defeating this whole gang but he was also getting his first clue as to who Silver was.

But he was quickly critical of his past gullibility in relation to her. She had always implied that some kind of ESP was her method of locating the various murders that she guided him to. Obviously, now, that was not a requirement. Since she was known to the gang, she obviously got her information by a mundane method. She was an insider. In fact, from the way Paul referred to her – could it be, was it possible, that she was Paul's wife?

Carl fought down a foolish moment of jealousy – he actually thought of it as foolish, for *him*, in *his* circumstances, to be jealous not only of his own wife, Marie, but of another man's wife. Nonetheless, there was a grimness in him as he surmised that the mysterious references to the 'ship' had an equally practical, underlying explanation.

Intent, determined, striving for a pragmatic attitude, he watched the scene in front of him.

The big man's lips had compressed. He was parting them to say something more, when there was a heavy pounding at the door. Paul nodded distractedly. 'All right,' he commanded, 'all of you start going out there to surrender. Henry and I will stay to the last, and keep phoning.' When no one moved, Paul's voice went up half an octave. 'Joe, you first; then you, Phil, Art, Peter and the rest of you.'

The naming of names established an order of precedence. The egress began. In the minutes that followed, Carl heard the front door open and close many times. Apparently, each time, one – and only one – member of the gang went outside. And the police were evidently quite happy to have them come at that sedate pace.

During those minutes, Henry called one after another of the people in his little notebook, and suddenly there was an answer. Henry spoke briefly to whoever it was, and then held the receiver out to Paul. 'Remember Ginsey?' he asked. The big man made a face, then said into the phone, 'Ginsey, here is your chance to rehabilitate yourself with the organization. Listen –' Quickly, he explained what had happened, and what he wanted – which was simply for Ginsey to continue trying to locate and advise certain persons. Whoever Ginsey was – whether man or woman – he (she) must have promised. For Paul replaced the receiver, stood for a long moment, and then followed Henry out into the hallway. Twice more, the front door opened and closed And there was silence.

Chapter Four

A THOUSAND VOICES FROM THE STARS

One minute and twenty-two seconds went by on the clock inside Carl. Then the distant front door opened. There was a rapid padding of soft rubber-soled shoes, and then four members of a police goon squad, in padded clothing and close-fitted helmets, rushed into the room.

They paused briefly to survey the two dead bodies. And one of them said, 'If Mabel could see me now.'

'Yeah,' said a second, 'that goes for Irma. She thinks her darling – that's me – is engaged in special police work. And, boy, I sure am. Go in first, and help take care of any tough guys that may still be lingering.'

'C'mon,' said a third, curtly, 'you know damn well both of you get a kick out of being goons. Let's go.'

The last speaker must have been in charge of the quartet. After his command, no more words were spoken. They started silently forward on their soft rubber shoes, and loped in single file through the alcove past Carl. They took with them his respect. No question, theirs was the preliminary dangerous task. Enter a risk area first. Be ready to grab, and hold, and fight. While a city slept peacefully, these men were doing their job in this violated house. Fortunately – Carl deduced – they would probably find no one.

He had no time to consider them further. Several uniformed police officers entered the room. After they, also, surveyed what was in the room, one of them picked up the phone, dialled, and said, 'Give me Captain Gates.' There was a pause; then: 'This is Lieutenant Turcott, sir. Two bodies here. So we'll be on this job for some time. Send the necessary, will you?'

He hung up, and mentioned to a plumpish aide in the uniform of a sergeant of police. 'Better call your wife now,' he said, 'while we're waiting, and the lines are clear.'

The plump man came forward sheepishly, picked up the phone dialled, and said, 'Hi, honey . . . Yeah, I'm in a house where a murder's been committed, and I'll be here probably until dawn on the details. That takes care of me for tonight . . . No, we captured a bunch of guys. They offered no resistance . . . Only the dead man here, and us cops. So you can go to sleep. G'night.'

He hung up, and visibly heaved a sigh of relief. 'Thanks, pal,' he said to Turcott. He made a gesture with his hands. 'I tell you that woman can't sleep until I phone.'

'No problem,' was the reply. 'I'm lucky. That's one difficulty I don't have with Martha. When she gets sleepy, she just has to lean towards the bed. After that she doesn't have time to think about what it's like for me to be in the homicide squad on the night shift.'

The routine police procedures that began presently took approximately two hours, at which time the bodies were carried out, and individuals began to leave. An hour after that, the lieutenant instructed two of his men to remain outside the house and keep a watch on it.

At this stage, only two police officers were apparently left in the house. One was Lieutenant Turcott, and the other, an older man – a grave-faced, forty-ish individual.

Turcott said, 'I'd like to see that machinery downstairs.'

'This way,' said the other. He added, 'It looks like a computer to me.' They walked out into the hallway, and Carl could hear them heading toward the rear of the house on the far side of the staircase.

About fifteen minutes went by, and then once more footsteps came closer. The two policemen re-entered the room, and this time it was the older man who, after glancing at his watch, said with an apologetic smile, 'I'll use that phone for a personal call, if you don't mind. Ingrid wants to be awakened by five o'clock, and it's almost that. She likes to be bathed, and perfumed, and made up, when I get home at 8:15.'

Turcott said in an incredulous tone, 'Three hours to get dressed!'

'She doesn't dress,' was the laconic reply.

Turcott's handsome face twisted into a moue of comprehension. He waved the man toward the phone, waited until the call had been made, and then said, 'I want to make one last check after everybody's gone.'

His companion said, 'I'll wait for you at the front door.' He walked off and out of sight.

Turcott had paused inside the hall door. From there he surveyed the room. His gaze lingered for several seconds on Carl but finally moved on and away.

He turned and departed. The front door banged shut for the last time.

Carl waited, as no less than three car motors started up outside, and there was the familiar sound of automobiles getting into motion. The sound faded into the distance.

Carl did not move immediately, because . . . What was my overall impression? – It was an old technique of his after a meeting: to review what had happened. Often, many insights emerged.

Abruptly, that happened again.

– The women, he thought, amazed.

Not a single woman had been present the entire night. Nevertheless, women had dominated the thoughts and attitudes of just about every male present. Including the policemen. Including – really – himself.

Carl was not actually surprised. It was an old theory of his that all human problems were female in origin.

Well-l-ll – modification: money and possessions were right in there. Money, and what it could buy. Property, the security it brought – and the women it attracted. Still, just about every male who wanted a woman could get some version of one. But not all men took the trouble, as he had done, to learn how to get money. So that was a vaguer impulse, except for some minimum eating and shelter requirements.

Okay – wearily – what now?

Carl rolled his six-wheeler over to where the single dead body had lain, when he first arrived. He looked down at that face again, this time in his mind's eye.

He had a difficulty then. The emotion that came was not one that he could recall ever experiencing before: compassion. Whoever the dead man was, he had refused to be

30

part of a plot. The refusal had cost him his life; and for a reason not clear that affected the one-time cold fish, Dr. Carl Hazzard.

The police had determined that his name was Jess Hodder; and he was a man who, apparently, had once accepted the tenets of the alienoids and their leader. It would be hard to decide what that leader, Paul, believed, and what he didn't. Cult bosses had to act *as if* they had special knowledge about what the organization stood for. Paul had come through effectively on that level. And, in fact, no question: Paul was a powerful personality.

As these additional awarenesses ran their courses through Carl, the emotion of regret that had briefly seized on him faded. Whereupon, he began to consider his own situation. What he wanted to do, would – he analyzed – have to be done carefully. The obstacle consisted of two constables who had been left to keep an eye on the house. Getting past them would take timing – and time.

While he waited for the two men to establish their routine, he searched for and found the stairway leading down to the basement . . . That machinery –

It was a broad and not at all ordinary type of basement stairway. Clearly, it had been built as a passageway for bulky objects; and Carl eased his six-wheeled 'self' down onto a concrete-floored corridor, which was filled up on one side all the way up to the ceiling with what looked like the massive metal switchboard of a large machine. The metallic panelling ran along the entire front to rear length of the house, about sixty feet.

Carl drove the full length, taking a quick look. His purpose: As a physicist who knew a lot about computers, he scanned the panelling for a company name or other markings that would identify the manufacturer and the make.

Nothing. No words . . . He returned more slowly, scanning for additional details. He had already noticed a control section. Now, he paused. First, he freed a jack cord from its receptacle in a little door in his own 'body.' Next, he reached up with one of his 'hand-arms' and plugged the jack into the top socket – one of several in the control panelling of the computer. As he had half-expected, the ohm-resistance was

31

many times different from what his own system was set for. And so he had to do a hasty job of switching from one resistor circuit to another until he achieved a matching effect.

He could only hope that the adjustment, rapid though it had been, had not registered on another control board somewhere; or, if it had, the control board had not been under observation during the crucial moments.

He forgot that. Something was coming through. His first awareness was, he had a sense of distance, as if he were on long-line telephone link-up. A faint echoing sound came from that distance, the kind of hum that was usually associated with a lot of energy.

The sound took on a shape in his brain. Something was stirring. An incredible, fantastic something. Colossal, super-human something.

The sound became a murmur of voices. Not only one voice. Many, incredibly many. Suddenly, a thousand voices were in his brain, speaking to him.

The 'something' seemed to sense that he was not capable of receiving such a quantity of information. The voices ceased. There was a pause. Carl waited, not knowing what to expect; and he was about to put his jack into the next-below socket, when –

A single voice said:

'From: Administrative Centre, To: Sub S, Logical Operation – Subject: Intruding Control Impulse. Message: "Urgently request investigation of unusual phenomenon affecting Command Core." '

Carl experienced a strong mental tension as he recognized that he was listening to machine message format. And, more important, the message indicated that his act of connecting himself to the computer had been detected.

Carl waited, not happy, startled by the speed of the detection system.

The initial steps of what followed were a simple procedure for whatever was doing the investigation. After only forty-three complex operations (each of which involved a mere thousand or so sub-operations) the analyzing unit decided that the intrusion derived from one of the three U.S.-based computers.

As it reached that conclusion, it said:

From: Administration Centre
To: Command Core
Subject: Intruding Control Impulse
Requested: Instructions for dealing with intruder
Recommended: Destruct.

At that precise instant, a somewhat awed – and partly convinced – Carl tugged his insert jack from the socket, and zoomed for the stairs. In all the minutes of flight that followed, he felt blank as to the real meaning of what he had heard. It seemed to him that, later, he could think about what it implied.

Chapter Five

THE CYCLE IS COMPLETED

The morning papers had arrived about two hours after Carl rolled into the Brain Room and connected himself to his various recharging units.

There was nothing on the front page. Not a word. Carl thereupon undertook the complicated – for him – task of leafing through each page of both papers. There was not a single reference to the arrests of the previous night.

At first it merely seemed improbable. Then he began to think of reasons ... The arrests had not been monitored in time to make the first editions. Yet already another memory was emerging. 'Ginsey,' he told himself, 'must finally have got hold of Gilbert, and Gilbert came down to the police station.'

It implied – political pull, control of newspapers, influence on the city, county, and even state level. Carl waited with a tiny hope for the second editions. But when they also had no mention of the previous night's events, he found that he was already resigned to the new reality.

Still didn't matter. But since he was a person who reasoned from cause to effect (where such applied) he had already had an unhappy thought.

At this point, he badly wanted to make a phone call; the question was, from where dare he make it? Not from a pay phone; too complicated for him except in an extreme emergency. So?

In the end, he put the call through the large switchboard in the main lab building. The hundred or so phones connected to it provided, not so much anonymity, as a barrier. If anyone came looking for him, he would have time to get away.

After he had made his request of the woman who intoned the words, 'Central Police Headquarters,' there

34

was a pause. Then a man's voice came on the line. 'Lieutenant Turcott is not in. Will someone else do?'

'No, it has to be he,' said Carl.

'Turcott,' was the reply, 'is ill and hospitalized. May I take a message?'

'Can you give me his home phone number?' Carl persisted.

'Just a moment.'

As the moment this time lengthened, Carl decided that they were trying to trace the phone that he was calling from. Regretfully, he hung up ... Okay, he thought, so they have the same feeling about Turcott as I have.

A key figure, Turcott, whom they would want to dispose of.

Carl was a man in a hurry now. Because, of course, for this he bore some responsibility. He might deduce that the alienoids had their own intent to destroy the officer. And that his inquiry would only hasten the action. But, still, it *could be* no murder purpose existed until he phoned.

The gang knew, or would shortly know, that two outsiders were involved. They must already have been apprized that a woman had phoned in the alarm the previous night, and brought an innocent police group down on their heads. And they would undoubtedly soon learn that a man's voice had asked about the principal police officer – an innocent who had acquired frightfully valuable information like names and addresses of the arrested people.

So they knew that a man and a woman ... at least ... were meddling. Confronted by the implications of that, the alienoids would waste no time.

Carl wasted none, either.

He asked for, and got, an outside line. He thereupon called the first Turcott listed in the central phone book. Then the second, then the third –

His question each time: 'Is this the home of Police Lieutenant Turcott?'

To his developing disconcertment, the answer was 'No' every time. 'Okay,' he thought, when this was established, 'so he lives in the suburbs –'

35

He obtained the four main outlying phone books, and went through those listings. There, also, with one exception, the answer was, 'No.' The exception was a Barry Turcott who lived on Sander Street in the outlying community of Keys. When he called Barry, a voice came on, and said mechanically, 'You have called a disconnected number.'

It was pretty baffling.

What made Carl persist was that the ... alienoids ... were remorseless. And would try to destroy all clues that might enable someone to trace them. Lieutenant Turcott was such a clue. They would move swiftly. He must also.

It was a bright, clear day, as Carl drove along in his panel truck. His destination: the suburban address of the Barry Turcott whose phone had been disconnected.

A wild chance. But – where else?

Somehow, Carl visualized that higher-ups in the phone company had conspired to divert calls such as his from the Turcott phone. His belief, quite simply, was that Barry had been disconnected for incoming calls shortly after dawn.

As he drove, he still had no idea how he, a mobile brain encased in a sizable six-wheeled vehicle, would be able to make the necessary inquiries in broad daylight.

The Sander Street address, it developed, was a neat little white house. It had a two bedroom look about it, and it was set back from the street on a fairly wide lot. There was a driveway that led to a rear garage; and two small boys about age five and three respectively were playing in the front yard.

Carl drove past, as if he were an ordinary truck on routine business. He deduced from the similar appearance of the neighbouring houses that he was in a housing development. A medium low income area, obviously. With one exception, the cars on the street were the smaller kind. The exception was a long, black Cadillac that was parked at the curb three hundred feet beyond the Turcott house. Two men sat in the front seat. Carl's scanning lens tried to get a look at them as he drove by, but the men had turned their heads away as he approached, and kept them turned.

Carl made a right at the next cross street, and he was

36

thinking, very simply, and even starkly, that it was possible he had arrived on the intended murder scene barely in time. And that accordingly, total boldness was indicated.

He did a complete 'circle', and turned onto Sander Street again a few minutes later. His vague hope that the black car would have departed was shattered as soon as he was able to see the full street. There it was, with the two men still in it.

As he approached the little white house once more, Carl was electrified to see that the big machine had backed a full two hundred feet closer to the Turcott place.

'Okay,' he thought grimly, 'so I'm going to jump to the conclusion that Turcott is actually in the house, and that they are after him; and that the battle is going to take place within minutes.' There were things he could do to prove that. But first, get those kids inside the house!

He drove purposefully forward, and parked at the kerb opposite the little boys. Through his outside speaker system, he called, 'Hey, kids!'

The boys looked up from their play. Presumably what they saw was a man sitting at the wheel of a panel truck. Carl had manipulated the head of the dummy driver, so that he seemed to be gazing toward the yard. Normally, a person in the front of a car trying to communicate to someone outside, would be leaning across the seat, and of course, normally what people said inside a car was not audible at any distance unless the speaker spoke very loudly.

But only adults, not boys, would be aware of such auditory problems. These boys came to the fence.

'Whatchawant?' asked the older.

'Is your father a policeman?' asked Carl.

He waited, tense. Had he been capable of breathing, he would have held his breath.

'Naw,' said the boy.

The mixed feeling that Carl experienced at that moment included both disappointment and relief. Stunning, how wrong one could be. The long black car, and its two men, and their behaviour – so incongruous in a community like this –

Yet with a single contemptuously-voiced negative, a

five-year-old boy had made all those significant appearances meaningless and made them appear to be the product
of his overstimulated imagination.

Carl's relief took account of the fact that the danger to
the two children was, in fact, non-existent. Therefore, no
problem with them.

The disappointment was keener. He was back where he
had started. The lost Lieutenant Turcott, with all his
knowledge, was for him as misplaced as ever. Meanwhile,
the enemy had learned where he was, and would be able to
seek him out with no interference –

The older boy was speaking again. 'My father,' he said
proudly, 'is a police *lieutenant*, not just an ordinary
policeman.'

Carl thought with a mental equivalent of a sigh, that the
perversity of human nature started early indeed.

Aloud, he said, 'Is your father home?'

'Yep, he's inside.'

The seconds were racing by, and yet every word still
needed to be enunciated without regard for the fact that
one of the two men had climbed out of the big car; and
without taking into account that the other one sat in the
seat in a peculiar, twisted way that concealed something
he held in his hand. This second man was leaning out of
the window on the kerb side, where Carl couldn't see what
he was up to.

But he guessed that the man held an energy weapon,
and with it was covering his companion who had now
started to walk toward Carl and the Turcott house.

Carl said, 'Listen, kid, take your brother, and go inside,
and tell your father to come out here. You and your
brother stay in the house, understand? Now, quick, get
your father.'

It was a sharp-toned adult voice, and the little boy was
suddenly scared. He grabbed the smaller child, and started
to run. As he reached the door, he burst into tears. Carl,
with his amplified listening devices turned up, could hear
him crying, 'Daddy, there's a man out there –' The boy
must at that moment have gone through to a second room,
for his words muffled suddenly.

38

Carl's brain did the equivalent of a hand movement that pushed a button which triggered a relay. With a tiny hissing sound, two panels in the roof of his truck folded back lengthwise. Simultaneously, the metal case which held the gun on top of his own 'body' slid away. The gun raised itself slightly only; he didn't want it to be visible just yet.

But he was ready.

The key moment came.

The front door of the little house opened. A young man came out. He was not in uniform.

Incredibly, that surprised Carl.

It was ridiculous, and a stereotype. In his mind, a police officer wore a uniform. During the prolonged moment while Carl adjusted to the reality that this police officer didn't, he was vaguely aware that the man who had set forth from the Cadillac had now arrived at the Turcott yard.

. . . A little startling, then, to realize that the two assassins intended to ignore whoever was in the panel truck. But still, in a world where small-vehicle drivers were normally unarmed and harmless, and not capable of interfering – sharp, purposeful minds observed, and by-passed, and trusted to lack of quick perception, and anticipated confusion.

The alienoid stopped almost directly in front of the truck, and stood with his back to Carl. He said to the young man in the yard, 'Are you Police Lieutenant Barry Turcott?'

'Why – yes,' was the reply.

'I have something for you,' said the stranger. He put his hand into his pocket.

It was the second stereotype; and once more it was distracting. *'I have something for you'* did not normally refer to death. In fact, what Carl reacted to was the hand movement. A man who reaches suddenly into his pocket in a moment of crisis cannot expect to complete the action unscathed.

What came out of the pocket was a small metal object. It resembled what Paul had used the previous night to kill Williams. When Carl saw that, he reacted. The thought he had in that instant set in motion a much faster mechanism than any human muscles would ever equal.

The computer aiming device of the cannon on top of Monty responded to that thought. The long rifle lifted on its oiled gear, and fired in one continuous movement. Since the rifle had a silencer attachment, the sound was a muffled plop.

Nevertheless, it was a bad moment; for the alienoid screamed. Hideously. And clutched the hand that had held the glinting thing.

The weapon had been lifted by the bullet and carried forward, and was lying on the ground inside the yard.

It was all pretty fantastic in that peaceful little community, and the first consequences began to show. Along the street people began to come out of their houses.

During those several moments of confusion, Lieutenant Turcott had produced his policeman's revolver from a hidden holster. He now brandished this weapon at the little panel truck, and said in a firm voice, 'Come on out of there, quick!'

It was the obvious thing for a police officer to do. It took no account of the deadly situation from which whoever was 'in' the panel truck had saved him. He was an agent of the law, and his duty was to take into custody friend or foe alike, if they broke the law.

Possession of a small cannon was unquestionably against that law.

He stood there on the sidewalk, and spoke again in the same determined voice, 'Come on, now, out – or I'll fire a bullet into one of your tyres.'

Carl said, 'Lieutenant Turcott, what happened to you after you arrested those men last night?'

There was a long pause. The question must have been extremely distracting, as if he were thinking rapidly, trying to fit *this*, which was happening, into *that*. Suddenly:

'That'll be the day,' said Lieutenant Turcott, 'when I give out that kind of information –'

Carl swung the rifle barrel around to point at the officer. 'Get into this car,' he commanded.

He had to believe that the large bore automatic rifle

40

looked formidable. All by itself it must make an impression of adequate, and therefore almost infinite, threat.

It was a sudden decision on his part. Truth was that there was no turning back. He had come out here to look over the situation, to inquire, to establish the officer's identity. Somehow he had believed that the assassination would not be attempted until night. Instead, he had arrived barely in time ... The killers had come in broad daylight, leaving him no alternative.

Having defended, having been seen, he was committed.

Lieutenant Turcott seemed to be frozen where he stood. Then he said shakily, 'You wouldn't shoot a gun like that at a human being?'

'I've already done so,' said Carl. *'Get in!'*

It must have been exactly as convincing as Carl imagined it to be. The rigid body of the young man did a peculiar giving-in gesture. And without a word, then, he walked forward, opened the door on the passenger side of the front seat, climbed in, and closed the door.

For the police officer, it must have been an interesting few moments, then. Standing outside, he must have thought that the dummy figure in the driver's seat was a real person. Not that easy to make out the interior through the slightly dirty glass ... deliberately made to appear grimy so it would always be hard to see into the vehicle from outside.

But, at this instant, awareness must have come to the lieutenant.

Carl would have liked to observe the discovery with him. But as the door closed, and Turcott seated himself, Carl put the little truck into motion, and headed for the Cadillac.

That was next, and not a pleasant conversation with a surprised policeman, who had just found out that he was in a car without a living driver in sight.

The outside scene was a bright sky, a street that still had no other cars on it, a few people standing on their porches looking toward the Cadillac, and toward Carl. Carl guessed that the onlookers could not possibly have a clear idea of what had happened or what was about to happen.

So he ignored them. Instead, he put his entire attention on the second man.

That individual took one look at the approaching vehicle, and made a dive for the open door – on the sidewalk side – of the long, black machine. Since Carl did not try to stop him, the man made it safely and proceeded to hastily roll up the windows.

Carl drew up opposite the big car, turned up the volume in his speaker system, and roared, 'Did Paul send you?'

Hastily, the short, dark individual inside the car rolled down the window, and said, 'For God's sake, tone that down. Who are you?'

Carl cut the volume. 'Are you married?' he asked.

The man's face twisted. For a moment, he looked blank. Then a grim smile crinkled his lips. He was visibly recovering, as he said, 'That's the damnedest question I ever heard at a time like this. But, yes, I'm married.'

'Does your wife,' asked Carl, 'know you're out on a dirty deal like this?'

Pause; then: 'No, she thinks I'm in my office.'

'Which is where?' asked Carl.

'Go to hell!' said the man in a tone of voice that was almost goodnatured.

Carl was delighted. The line of questioning, sort of assuming humanness, had occurred to him suddenly; but it was a direct outgrowth of his night-before insight that the alienoids *and* the police officers had both shown that close to the surface of their thoughts was a woman.

He had a feeling that that awareness, which had now been stimulated, would dominate every future moment of this dialogue. He pressed on, 'Were you at the Hodder house last night?'

'I don't know what you're talking about,' he replied curtly.

Well, maybe he didn't know. Carl didn't remember seeing this particular person. Not that that proved anything. Several people there he hadn't seen clearly.

'Were you sent by somebody to kill Lieutenant Turcott?'

'I couldn't possibly answer a question like that without benefit of counsel.'

42

'Look,' said Carl flatly, 'I've got a gun here that can tear you and your machine apart, and you'll never get home to your wife if I do. But I don't plan to turn you over to the police. I want information.'

Pause. Narrowed eyes glared at him. Teeth showed from between lips. Then: 'I don't know who you are, my friend. But, yes, Paul sent me. Yes, we *were* here to kill Lieutenant Turcott – though I, personally, considered it an unnecessary precaution in view of what's about to happen.'

'You mean unnecessary because the ship is coming.' Carl spoke tentatively. The ship was not something he had given thought to; but he had a feeling that this cult group believed something about it. So he spoke the meaningless words.

The pause this time was shorter. 'Am I –' he urgently uttered – 'talking to another Secret?'

'Secret what?' asked Carl.

'Friend,' said the man, 'if you're a Luind, your leader is to be advised of the details tomorrow morning. So don't do anything rash now. And that's all I'm going to say.'

Carl instantly accepted the finality of it. And, besides, it was time. He said, 'Listen carefully: pick up your companion – his hand is hurt – and be out of here by the time I turn around at the next corner.'

His rear view of the 'companion' showed a fairly pitiful scene. The man was standing in a crouching position holding his shattered right hand with his left. Carl could only guess that one or more fingers had been shot off. The peculiar, twisted fashion in which the man held his body indicated extreme pain. He definitely needed emergency medical care.

As he guided the panel truck to the near corner, he saw, looking rearward, that the second man was indeed following instructions. The Cadillac swayed into motion – and came to an abrupt stop near the injured man.

The driver leaned out then, and he must have yelled something – though that was impossible to hear from where Carl was. However, the information was conveyed. The would-be killer staggered around to the side of the car,

43

and, as the other man opened the door for him, he half fell, half crawled, inside.

Seconds later, the Cadillac was on its way as Carl made a U-turn, and started back the way he had come.

'All I want,' he said to Turcott, 'is the name and if possible the address, of the man called Paul and the man called Henry. If you name them for me, and I believe you, I'll pull up opposite your house, and let you out.'

He added earnestly, 'Those men were sent to kill you, as you heard. So no matter what I do you'd better take evasive action.'

To Carl, it seemed perfectly logical, what happened then. Any police officer in his right mind would be attracted by the idea of escaping from an enforced situation.

There was a long pause. Then: 'What do you intend to do to those men – Paul, Henry?' asked the officer in a quiet voice.

'I want to talk to them. I don't intend to harm them.'

Another pause, shorter this time. Then with a sigh, 'Every man in that round-up,' said Lieutenant Turcott, 'was a member of a prominent, wealthy family. Paul is *the* Paul Gannott of the banking family. Henry Granville is the international jewelry firm.'

'Were they released?'

'Yes.'

'There will be no further questioning?'

'Their story was accepted after certain persons intervened,' said the police officer in an even voice, 'and the two deaths are listed as suicides.'

They had come up opposite the house. Carl pulled over to the kerb. He said, 'Why don't you take your little family, and go on a trip. Leave within two hours –'

He stopped. There was a look on the young man's face, as seen in Carl's front seat viewer. 'I'm sorry,' said Turcott, 'Martha can't be moved from anywhere to anywhere in two hours.'

Carl recalled Turcott using that name the night before. But he checked anyway. 'Martha – your wife?'

'Yes.'

44

'She wouldn't move even to save your life?'

'It wouldn't be real to her fast enough. Of course –' grim smile – 'she'd be regretful afterwards. But right now, she'd probably want me to call the local police.'

Carl thought: Martha – Marie – the two names and personalities seemed to have a certain unhappy similarity ... For God's sake, why are these females all so rigid? – At least (with satisfaction) I stood up to Marie all these years, and told her where she could go.

Unfortunately, she had not gone. And, in staying, she had given him fourteen years of exactly nothing. So it wasn't a victory ... Funny, how he could finally have accurate thoughts like this after all this time.

The brief reverie ended as Turcott said, 'Fact is, in listening to that conversation, I have the impression the danger is over for me. Nobody is going to be sent after me until they find out who's behind you.'

– I'll be damned, thought Carl ... He immediately had the same feeling. He said, 'But be careful for a couple of days. And, right now, if that little weapon is still on your lawn, will you get it and put it in here? I'd like to examine it later.'

The young man stepped down, walked into his yard, stooped, straightened, came back, tossed a metallic-looking object onto the floor of the cab part of the van, drew back, and slammed shut the door of the truck.

'If I need you,' he said, 'where can I reach you?'

Pause. Silence.

Carl was thinking that the truth was he no longer believed the alienoids were his killers ... But I can act if I wish – He had the names of the two leading members, Paul and Henry.

The proof of their non-involvement was all that publicity at the time when he was run down and his body destroyed. For some reason Silver hadn't seen the news reports. But, surely – *surely* – in a group of ten or more people somebody would have done something.

But they hadn't cared that his brain was saved. Had paid no attention. To them it had been as if he did not exist.

Carl thought: The cycle is completed ... This was his second last act in the drama of the alienoids.

Naturally, one should take all possibilities into account; so he said, 'Well, lieutenant, I came out here to save your life. So I've accomplished my purpose, and you're on your own from now on. But,' carefully, 'if you ever want to get in touch with me for a good reason, place an ad in the personal column of either newspaper, and sign it B.T. And if I ever need to get in touch with you, I'll either get your phone number from information or put in an ad addressed to B.T. How's that?'

'Thank you, sir.'

Carl drove off, thinking that his last act must be to head off Silver, if possible. No point, really, in interviewing her now. Her sad little story was all too stereotyped – now that he knew she was aquainted with the alienoids as individuals.

For some reason, either the truth of that or else the decision to withdraw from the situation depressed him as he drove uneventfully home.

Chapter Six

CUTOFF IN THE BRAIN ROOM

Arrived at the laboratory, he parked his van, drove down the ramp, into the building, and headed for the Brain Room. As he rolled along one aisle, he was spoken to by an elderly maintenance man and a young physicist, and he replied in a minimum way. All around him was the clatter of machinery, the hissing of gasses, and the hum of electric motors starting and stopping. The laboratory's principal products were liquid oxygen and liquid hydrogen. Each process had its own sounds.

Once inside his own room, he allowed the tyres of his six wheels to settle in their grooves. And there he stayed.

And stayed. Sort of blank and unhappy, and a little puzzled. He had a long-time philosophy: one cannot bow out of life, because life does not let him. Somebody out there will show up and force even the most withdrawn types to react. If no one else comes, one day the tax collector knocks on the door.

Carl thought: – It looks as if, for me, that law of life could actually be suspended ... He literally didn't have to do anything. Even his taxes were being paid for him by duly authorized people.

As for the man-woman thing – usually the biggest inciter of all – it was for him the most nothing situation of all. True, Marie was out there in her fashion. But, fortunately – he felt fortunate – she was the 'good woman' type; and it took literally mountains to move a woman like that out of her timeless passivity.

So far as Carl could see there was not a mountain in sight.

Dr. Carl Hazzard, disembodied brain, feeling lulled in connection with his wife, waited for what he dully believed would be endless emptiness.

About twenty minutes went by.

The door to the Brain Room – which was unlocked daytimes – opened suddenly. Dr. Angus MacKerrie walked in, and closed the door behind him. Whereupon Carl, in effect, stirred. Which meant, simply, that he started to emerge from what he was doing, or rather not doing.

The surgeon walked forward slowly toward the machine that was Carl. And Carl studied him through his exteroceptive system ... The only man in the world, he thought, with proven skill to perform a brain transplant. And he moves around like an ordinary person, and drives through dangerous traffic, and is now over forty years old, and getting older –.

He was aware of MacKerrie pausing a dozen feet away.

The other stood there, then, seemingly pensive, a medium-tall man in a grey suit. He had bright grey eyes, and an even-featured face that showed the bare beginnings of middle age jowls.

If he had an inner life different from his professional life, there was no sign of it. He said, 'I got to thinking again about your remarks the other day – that matter of searching for your murderer – and it's been bothering me. Would you like to enlarge on that, and either relieve my mind, or tell me the worst, whichever?'

It cost Carl a distinct mental effort to turn his attention back to *that* ... What can I say to him quickly about my plan to find my murderer? It all seemed very far away right now, and not relevant. Yet he felt cautiously reluctant to express a mere negation or dismissal of the idea. As a scientist he had learned the hard way (in his youth) not to put forth an idea until he was fairly sure it was valid, and not to launch a project and then abandon it. Similarly, now, it would be wrong to admit that two days after mentioning such a search to MacKerrie he was already vague about it.

He said tentatively, 'I gather you're against such a search. You didn't object two days ago when I first told you.'

MacKerrie shrugged. 'You represent several million dollars and my skill. Think about it. As for objecting, I like

48

to think things over before putting in my nickel's worth. Anyway, here I am forty-eight hours later.'

Carl said quickly, 'I guess it's hard for people to take a bodiless brain seriously.'

'I take you seriously,' said MacKerrie in an even tone. He had heard variations of that complaint before. As an experimenter, he was immediately interested in learning if it was the same thought or a different one.

'A man without a body,' said Carl, 'and particularly a man without sexual ability is the most nothing person in the world.'

The surgeon said quietly, 'In olden times, eunuchs often became top military and administrative leaders. So the absence of sex doesn't seem to be a problem.'

'There I was,' said Carl, 'in process of making a detailed study of female behaviour, with particular reference to my wife's rejection of me. I can see now that some of my attitudes offended her justifiably, but at the time that didn't seem real to me. That study looks like a waste now.'

'The study of human nature has historically been partly done by old men past the age of sexual ability.'

'Marie was frigid for fourteen years,' he said plaintively.

'I've gathered from chance remarks,' said MacKerrie, 'that you were consistently unfaithful to her, but couldn't believe that should be a factor in her non-response.'

'I can see it now,' said Carl. 'How would you explain my change of understanding?'

'You probably knew it all the time, but didn't want to give up your masculine pleasures.'

'Yes and no –' Carl sounded puzzled. 'The "no" comes from the fact that I'd seen men who were openly on the make, whose wives had made their peace with that. At the time I thought Marie ought to be equally tolerant with me. Why wasn't she?'

'Good question,' said MacKerrie, noncommittally.

'The whole mystery of women's behaviour concerned me so much that I wrote a book on the subject. It was never published, and in fact never intended to be published. I titled it, *Women Are Doomed*.'

'I've heard references to the book but have never seen it.'

'What I meant was, how can a woman go fourteen years without sex? Surely, she should have an interest in the act for herself, not merely in relation to her husband. So that, if he offends her, she shouldn't just sit there blank.'

'It does seem wrong,' agreed MacKerrie. He broke off. 'All this seems very academic at present. What are you leading up to?'

'For this and other reasons,' said Carl in an arguing voice, 'women are doomed to live a relationship type of existence. Since that was true to me, in my scientific fashion I decided I would require her to live with her inner reality.'

'It has been observed,' said the surgeon, 'that a strict scientific approach does not work with human beings.'

'You're suggesting there's more to a woman than her automatic behaviour?'

'I'm suggesting,' was the reply, 'that, really, no science exists as yet; and that, clearly, you did not know enough factors for you to apply anything but an experimental method. From your account, my analysis would be that Marie did not respond as you predicted because your theory was not complete.'

Carl was suddenly gloomy. 'The worst part of it is, now that I can see my errors, it doesn't seem worthwhile my pursuing the study. The way I feel now, if I were to get my body back, I would simply say to her, "Look, Marie, I'm going to give up those other women. Can we start again?'

'That would certainly alter the original experiment, and reinstate a method worked out by society over the ages.' Once more MacKerrie attempted to change the discussion. 'Look, Carl –'

'Why did I and millions of men and some women rebel against that long-established societal system?' Carl demanded, 'and seek an equivalent of plural marriage?'

'I understood the answers to that were in your book, *Women Are Doomed*.'

'My observations in that book,' Carl replied, 'are true as far as they go. It could be that they miss what might be termed female consciousness –'

50

MacKerrie recognized the thought as new for Carl. 'Another automatic,' he analyzed aloud.

'But one that would pre-empt anything else, as a basic consciousness always does.'

'True.'

'The question becomes,' Carl urged, 'what is female consciousness?'

'I hate to say this to a scientist of your eminence,' said MacKerrie, 'but the real problem is not what is the question, but what are the questions?'

Carl sounded gloomy again. 'I suppose you're right. And the fact is, why am I still concerned in any way? My original reason for trying to solve the problem was designed to get Marie to lie down, in spite of the fact that I had several mistresses. Now, even if she were willing, it wouldn't do me any good. My feeling intent at present is the hope that she will remain frigid, so that I won't have to contend with jealousy.'

Since the surgeon had a positive knowledge that Marie had been compromised into having an affair – in his opinion a good thing for her – he changed the subject and said, 'Which brings me back to my earlier question. According to the gateman, you've been out on two fairly long jaunts. Where did you go?'

Momentarily, that brought a return of disinterest, an instant feeling that this was no longer relevant, a strong impulse to dismiss the question with the simple, partly true statement. 'I have an account on a tape –' But unfortunately he had not put it all on tape. That last part with Turcott was not recorded.

Carl was swiftly resigned . . . There's something about a direct question from a man on whom you are as dependent as I am on Mac – one either lied, or else told the questioner to mind his own business. In his day, he had done both without a qualm. But that was another time and another Carl.

With the decision thus taken away from him, he described his two experiences, succinctly but accurately.

For long seconds after the fantastic account was completed, MacKerrie was stunned. Finally, his memory began to trickle back. But the feeling of overwhelm dominated, and spoke first:

'B-but what are they, these alienoids?'

'A cult of wealthy men.'

'And this ship?'

Carl was contemptuous. 'They've got a computer that's been programmed to act like it's a ship far out in space, coming here from – I gather – another star system.'

'Oh!'

It was at once obvious that MacKerrie was not a man who believed in things like that.

He was frowning. 'You mean, some group of well-to-do nuts?'

'They're waiting for it as if it's the second coming of J.C.,' said Carl.

'B-but –' MacKerrie was bewildered – 'how did a man like you get involved in something as far out as that?'

'Sex – of course.'

The physician was abruptly critical. 'Carl, for heaven's sake, in a world where you with your money could get practically any woman you wanted, how could you possibly associate with a female who tolerates ideas like that?'

'She was beautiful.'

'How would you know? You never saw her, by your own account.'

'She *felt* beautiful.'

'For heaven's sake, Carl, you must have been out of your mind.'

'It's true,' confessed the brain that had once been a man.

By the time that reluctant admission was spoken, MacKerrie was calmed down again. But he was puzzled. 'I thought you believed Walter did it,' he said.

'Did what?'

'Murdered you.'

'Oh, that,' said Carl.

'How do you mean?' MacKerrie was puzzled. 'You practically had him in a mental institution from fear.'

'Walter!' Carl's tone was scathing. He went on in a dismissing tone, 'In those days it gave me a perverse pleasure to pretend that Marie was up to sexual excesses, though of course I know perfectly well that she hadn't had sex since about three months after we were married. Accusing Walter was a punishment of her for cutting me off way back there.'

The explanation made an unfortunate impression on MacKerrie. He had never previously made up his mind about the various reported behaviours of this brilliant, erratic genius. But –

The possibility of being publicly charged by Carl with murder had just about driven Dr. Walter Drexel out of his mind. In his desperate effort to control the situation, the man had – among other reactions – sought total control of Marie. Impotent himself, he had nonetheless required her to pretend to MacKerrie that he was her lover, on the threat that he would swear that Marie and he had indeed conspired to kill Carl. And, since MacKerrie knew of Carl's suspicion, Walter (in his panicky need to have a hold on the man) insisted that she become MacKerrie's mistress, also.

It had ever since been a source of mixed feelings for MacKerrie that he had decided it was best for Marie that he go along with such an enforcement. He was a man who could have many women; but never had more than one at a time. Because of his genuine affection for Marie he had given up his previous woman friend, so that there would be no conflict or degradation for anyone. And in his determined fashion – for her own good – had accepted her as his mistress.

She felt enforced. *He* believed that as a woman she had allowed herself to be destroyed by an unfaithful husband, and believed that she must be rescued from her timeless frigidity by someone who actually had her best interests at heart.

Unfortunately, he had mentioned to her that some aspect of giving Carl mobility had resulted in a personality change for the better. Instantly, the no-longer-threatened woman cut him off as her lover.

The cut-off was no problem to him. The world was full of good-hearted, trusting women who needed a man who never strayed and who stayed until she, in her invariable

53

developing disturbance, herself eventually broke off the relationship. The woman always wanted to be married. And of course, because his wife was in a mental institution, he couldn't. Wouldn't. Ever. If she ever came to, and needed him, he intended to be there, instantly available.

For some reason, in the final issue, a woman refused to understand, or condone, or accept, his obligation to an insane wife ... Their refusal had taught him things about women.

Under the circumstances ... nothing he could do for them, except go as they demanded.

Here, it was different. Because of Carl he couldn't just silently steal away into the night ... Something to think about, and decide later. Right now –

Carl – what to do about him? ... This man, he thought, could endanger my whole brain experiment by taking one fantastic risk after another – It was all very brave, but very reckless ...

Standing there, MacKerrie made up his mind that he needed time to think about the best course. He said, 'I'd like to do a little maintenance on you to see how you came through your two journeys.'

The man-brain felt no suspicion. In fact, it sounded like very good sense. 'Go ahead,' he replied, 'and, Mac, now please don't tell Marie what I've just told you.'

'Of course not,' said MacKerrie.

Half an hour later, MacKerrie withdrew from the inner workings of the six-wheeled vehicle. He seemed breathless. He said, 'Well, everything appears to be okay. We'll have to keep a close watch.' He headed for the door and opened it. 'I've suddenly realized I have an appointment. See you.'

'Hey, wait!' said Carl. 'You didn't reconnect –'

The roar of the factory pouring through the open doorway overwhelmed his words.

The door shut. The huge noise collapsed. But MacKerrie was gone.

Normally, in leaving Hazzard Laboratories, MacKerrie would have gone to his car in the parking lot inside. And then he would drive out through the gate. But he had a strong conviction that Dr. Carl Hazzard would already have called the gateman in an effort to intercept his departure. MacKerrie went instead to the house. There, he discovered from Mrs. Gray something which he already knew – that Marie was somewhere in the laboratory.

The man said hastily, 'I won't wait. Just let me out the front door.'

Out on the street, safely away, MacKerrie hailed a cab. As he was driven away, he wondered if Carl would phone Marie and tell her that MacKerrie had inadvertently disconnected him from control of his six-wheeled vehicle.

In the Brain Room, Carl's initial agitation faded rapidly. He decided very swiftly not to involve Marie. And so – he told himself – it was simply a matter of waiting peacefully until he could contact MacKerrie. Which – he believed – would surely be not later than the next day.

And, in fact, he *was* peaceful until shortly after nine p.m. that night.

Chapter Seven

CAPTIVE OF THE ALIENOIDS

Peace ended when an automatic relay closed inside Carl. It was a circuit which normally connected him to the protective electrified fence that surrounded the laboratory grounds; and its message to him was that the electricity had shut off.

Carl stirred out of his quietness ... and his intercom phone rang. It was the outside gate guard, reporting that there had been a cut-off of electricity to the protective fence. The harsh voice concluded, 'I have no instruction about such a cut-off. It's on a separate meter. What do you advise?'

The man-brain was now definitely startled ... Is this accident? Or design?

He managed to say, 'Call the electric company, and ask for emergency service.'

Having spoken, he broke the connection. He waited there, and he thought that, logically, it had to be a coincidence.

The intercom phone rang. Peters said, 'My outside phone is dead, sir. Will you phone the electric company?'

'Of course,' said Carl.

First, he tried to phone out through the laboratory switchboard. When there was no dial tone, he – second – tried to phone on his private outside line, the one Silver had called him on. No dial tone.

This, decided Carl, is ridiculous. Obviously, though, it couldn't mean anything sinister. In his precise fashion, he brought to mind a conversation he'd had with a phone company engineer a few years back. At the time there had been a problem with an employee suspected of dishonesty. It turned out that no matter how swiftly an alert phone technician was advised that the man was phoning out, he could not trace the call during the few minutes the suspect was on the line.

And that's all the alienoids had had that morning, when he'd called the police station: two minutes, no more. So it was impossible that they had tracked him down.

Still . . . check.

He reconnected with the gateman. 'Who else is on the premises, Peters?' he asked.

'Your wife, her housekeeper, and the laboratory watchman, sir. Dr. MacKerrie is sleeping at the Brain Foundation tonight, instead of in his cottage at the rear.'

'Oh, yes.' Unhappily, Carl recalled his phone call in the wee hours after Silver called, and the recorded reply from Mac.

Since the two watchman were armed, Carl presumed that they could take care of themselves. As for Marie, during his courtship of her, he had taught her to fire a pistol. But now he had a frustrated feeling that if Marie were suddenly required to locate the .25 calibre automatic he'd given her, she wouldn't be able to.

That incredible woman, he thought. She'll be the only problem in a crisis, I'll bet . . .

Should he call her and warn her? It seemed too soon. Marie didn't react well to anxiety. She usually worried twice as much as a threat called for. Better wait and make sure, before putting that kind of strain on her.

'Sir,' said the hoarse voice of Peters, 'take a look at section 3-N.'

3-N was the western part of the north fence. As Carl focussed his remote control TV on the indicated section, he saw a man's head was peering over the fence into the grounds. Presumably, the intruder was standing on a step ladder.

As Carl watched, the intruder edged up until he was kneeling on the concrete top. Then, while holding onto one of the strands of wire (which was normally electrified), he reached back and down – and drew up a ladder. It was evidently made of one of the light metals, for he swung it up over the highest wire; held it there, then climbed over himself, and finally lowered it until its bottom touched the ground inside the fence; all done with great ease.

There seemed to be a moment of imbalance as his foot somewhat blindly sought for the top rung. It took him a measurable time to steady himself, but presently he began to descend, as the head of a second man peered over the fence.

Carl watched, helpless to do anything ... If they manage to get inside this room, I won't even be able to defend myself – that was what he'd better decide about; if they broke in to where *he* was, what to do about that?

The severity of the danger astounded him. Incredibly, in this crisis he was completely disconnected from all of the equipment of his six-wheeled support vehicle, including the big rifle. As the appalling realization came that he would have to sit here and await events, he did manage a rueful thought: There goes my longstanding theory, that crises in human affairs are only caused by the side effects of the man-woman thing ...

Clearly not relevant here; so it seemed to Carl.

During those rapid moments, while he considered his predicament, the second man started down the ladder, a third straddled the wires, and the head of a fourth peered from behind the far side of the wall.

As Carl watched, Number Two reached the ground and ran off to one side, Number Three came down and ran in another direction; numbers four, five, and six took equally swift, evasive action. Altogether, in the next ten minutes, Carl counted thirty-eight intruders.

And that seemed to be the invading force.

Time to act. Which meant it was time to decide what the other people on the grounds should do. No time to do anything for himself except figure out some way whereby no one noticed him.

Carl called Peters on the intercom. Once, twice, three times.

No reply. Good God! Moments later, when the intercom call to Marie also went unanswered, Carl suffered a reversion to an old impatience.

He visualized Marie sitting in her bed, reading. And

refusing to answer the phone. In her time, she had done a thousand maddening things like that . . . In a minute, Mrs. Gray would pick up the phone, but, meanwhile, what a waste of vital time.

The minute went by; and Mrs. Gray did not lift the receiver, either.

While he considered that, and felt suitably baffled, Carl switched over to a view of the interior of the laboratory. Silence. Long, dimly lighted aisles between dark rows of darkly gleaming machinery. Still deserted – no, wait!

Over by one of the storage rooms, flashlights winked. Several hard-to-see men were retreating from the locked door of that room.

The next second: a sharp explosion. A flash of flame from the door . . . By God, they've knocked out the lock.

Instantly, Carl had his own optimum solution. The one thing he had been able to do before he was mobile was unlock his own door. He unlocked it now, hastily, thinking: When they come to my room, and find the door unlocked, they'll begin with the assumption that there's nothing important inside; and when they come in I'll be just another machine standing here . . .

It turned out to be a false analysis. The half-dozen men who entered the Brain Room eight minutes later paused to survey the considerable machinery inside. After moments only, one of them gestured at Carl with his thumb. Without a word being spoken, all the men moved purpose-fully over, eased Carl out of the wheel slots he was settled into, and rolled the six-wheeled vehicle that contained him through the open door, along several silent aisles, and up a ramp into the capacious rear end of a truck that had backed through the unguarded outside gate. He had time to see that the van with the rifle was in the forward part of the big interior of the truck.

Swiftly, wide holding straps laced him against one side of the truck's inside, and the ramp folded up and became the truck's rear door. The machine started to move forward. Carl was aware when it went over the bump and down-incline that led to the street.

He could feel it turn right, toward the nearby freeway entrance. Within minutes it was racing along at freeway speeds; and it was presently evident that he had been successfully captured.

Chapter Eight

SPACESHIP IN THE SKY

Earlier –

Marie's intercom phone rang . . . Carl, she thought, and let it ring. Moments later the faint sound of footsteps outside her apartment heralded Mrs. Gray, who said, 'A Colonel Nicer is on the line.'

Puzzled, Marie picked up her receiver. 'How did you get on our intercom?' she asked.

'I'm calling from the gate,' was the low-voiced reply – the tone was instantly electrifying – 'We have just taken the gateman here, and the factory watchman, into protective custody.' His voice changed, and he spoke again before she could react to the astounding information. 'Dr. Marie,' he said earnestly, 'this place is in process of being attacked by a considerable force. Can you and Mrs. Gray get dressed, and go separately in two cars that will drive up to your street door in five minutes?'

'Attacked!' echoed Marie at that point, faintly.

She had a wild thought the next instant: – Is this his way of putting pressure on a woman he is courting . . . The mere possibility was staggering. The most fantastic method she had ever heard of.

'The alienoids are coming,' said Nicer's voice, 'and right now we're disconnecting the intercom. So quick! And don't worry about Dr. Carl. He knows what's going on, and as you're aware he's mobile. I'll call you when it's over. Goodbye.'

Marie gasped, 'The who is coming?' She felt blank. Alienoids? There was a click. She was speaking to a vacated line.

As she dressed with frantic haste, she was remembering the board meeting only two mornings ago of the Non-Pareil Corporation. She represented Carl, the former president

61

and the largest stockholder. Like the other directors, she had sat at a gilt table, and couldn't help but notice that all of the three other women present were younger and prettier than herself. There was Tina Glay, a blue-eyed stunner, whose husband was a vice-president (but out of the country, so she represented him). And of course, as always, also on hand was Melina Malagini, the beautiful woman with the ever-narrowed eyes, who attended all board meetings with her husband, who – people believed – invariably voted according to her judgment and not his own. And last, among the women was Ms. Craig, thirty-six years old, heiress to her late parents' stock. A few years before, on hearing of Carl's book on women (which he had titled, *Women Are Doomed: the Aphorisms of Carl Hazzard*), she had calmly announced a book project of her own, coincidentally titled, *Men Are Doomed*.

Carl was not amused, although he did laugh scornfully on several occasions. And a few times in Marie's presence he had asked in his most ironic voice for a progress report on the work. 'Put me down,' he had said, 'for the first copy to come off the printing press.'

In her conversations with Carl, Kyra Craig had always been very calm. In connection with the progress of the writing, she invariably said, 'It's coming fine.' As far as any difficulties were concerned, she had reported, 'The hardest section to be objective about has to do with the aphorisms on Real Men.' In reference to his request to purchase a copy, she had always stated, 'My book will not be for sale to men. It will be available to women only.'

There was another drama in which Kyra Craig played a role. She was playing it this morning in front of Marie's eyes. Kyra was carefully avoiding looking at the man who sat across the table from Marie. As Marie vaguely recalled it, this individual had as a youth been Kyra's first fiance, when she was still in her late teens. The engagement had been in that long ago broken for reasons unknown to outsiders. But, since then, Ms. Craig had been married three times. Her current husband was a movie producer and a rather nice guy.

This particular shareholder's presence was actually quite

an event. Marie hadn't seen him since he had gone off to Viet Nam in the late sixties. This unexpected person was Philip Nicer, only 'child' (approximately her own age) of another deceased vice-president. As Marie noticed him, and nodded recognition, he nodded back with a faint smile. But in addition his gaze momentarily locked with hers. She had a startled impression of being evaluated in a single lightning appraisal. Then the eyes, which were grey, turned away, thoughtful.

As the meeting neared its finale, the president – who had formerly been the financial expert of the organization – introduced the sharp-eyed Philip as 'not only one of the leading shareholders of Non-Pareil but as Colonel Nicer of U.S. Intelligence, who has some important data for us.'

Marie was impressed. Colonel! she thought. Why, that's next to General – The once nice young man had gone far, indeed.

Colonel Philip Nicer, when he stood up, was five feet ten inches and slender; and his voice, when he spoke, had a determined vibrance in it. He said that it was the belief of Military Intelligence that extra vigilance had again become necessary at all staff levels. 'Somebody – we don't know who – is infiltrating all major space manufacturers. Our task, of course, is to find out who these people are, and who is behind them.' He particularly urged board members, who were also working officers, to re-evaluate long-time key people.

After his brief speech, Nicer came straight over to Marie – which was a little startling. But she was (she had to admit it) charmed. For about one minute. Then she got the gist of what he was saying.

He wanted to come over to Hazzard Laboratories and interview a dozen key people, including Carl and MacKerrie and several scientists, all of whom he named. That startled her. Names, she knew, were not easy to come by in a world as full of people as an Intelligence officer's world must be. One had to be sincerely inquisitive to have that information at one's tongue tip.

'And –' Nicer completed his series of requests – 'when I've talked to those individuals, I should like to drop by your official residence and have a discussion with you about, let's see –' he pursed his lips, tilted his head, smiled, and continued '– about transactional psychology in personal relations.'

He knows! About her affair with MacKerrie (even though it was now ended). About the fact that Carl had threatened to accuse Dr. Walter Drexel of murdering him; and of Walter's threat to implicate her – all that – she realized suddenly had been in Nicer's appraising glance minutes before.

The shock was so great that Marie didn't react by moving. She reacted by continuing to sit very still. After what was to her an indeterminate time, she had a wry rememberance of one of the old Carl's aphorisms from his unpublished work, *Women Are Doomed:* 'The fate of a beautiful woman in trouble is to be passed around from man to man on an exact transactional basis.'

Marie was taken to a hotel in the Wilshire district in a military car driven by a man in uniform. The room she was taken to was of the high quality that she was accustomed to. For a while she lay on the bed fully dressed, tense and anxious. But finally she thought: – Okay, so perhaps he has a key to this room also. But the truth is, he's a gentleman. I'm sure he'll phone first and ask my permission to come up. I can decide then whether or not to let him . . .

With that, she undressed, slipped in under the sheets, thought: – The fact is, I am receiving the special care that goes with the transaction he offered me, and I might as well realize it . . . and she slept as she was having the thought.

Marie struggled out of sleep – and realized what the problem was. Fuzzily, she grabbed at the phone, which was ringing in short bursts, typical of some hotel switchboard operators.

'Hello,' she murmured.

'Did I awaken you?' said the voice of Philip Nicer. He spoke in an oddly cosy, personal way.

Marie had fumbled the bedside light on by this time, and had had a glimpse of her watch: Ten to four . . . Eeeee! . . .

64

Then: – It must be over, she thought. The attack, everything.

'*What happened?*' The question flowed out of her in a single breath.

'I'm downstairs,' Nicer said. 'May I come up?'

What happened then was not exactly a pause. It was a process of thought. The thing that amazed Marie was that no words had been spoken by him or by her that implied what was now only a single word away from fruition. No proposal had been made, and none received. The entire dialogue that had ever passed between them, if written down, would in no way appear to mean what it was now obviously meaning. And which of course she, and he also, had clearly understood it to have meant.

The rapid awareness, all in the space of a breath or two, changed the situation.

The truth was she was not a woman who was available for swift affairs. Or, normally, for *any* at all.

The thought-feeling about that had been forcing itself to the surface of her mind almost from the first moment of awakening. And with it a sense of –

Something very complex. In Marie, at that instant, a thousand barriers sprang, so to speak, into 'ready' position. The sum and essence and meaning in that solid mass had her say now:

'Really, Colonel – at this hour?'

'I'll be damned,' said Philip Nicer.

As the man uttered the exclamation, there was a faint stirring of regret in Marie; a conviction that she ought not to let this be the end. Thinking thus, she said quickly, 'Why don't we have breakfast together?'

The man's voice at the other end seemed to have recovered when he spoke again. For he said quietly, 'I have a 7:45 meeting. So why don't you join me for breakfast at 6:30.'

'I'll be there,' said Marie. She spoke eagerly, aware that something was wrong, but held completely helpless from within. The breakfast seemed a way out, a suitable substitute.

They had their breakfast together shortly after dawn in

a cafe across from the hotel (the hotel coffee room, it turned out, did not open until 7:30 a.m.) From the moment that they sat down, Marie noticed that Nicer had a faraway look in his eyes, and that he kept glancing at his watch. He seemed to find it difficult to put his attention on her.

From this she drew the conclusion, correctly or incorrectly, that he had never been interested in her as a person but only as a woman ... So I was right, she thought, right, right to do what I did.

She didn't notice that it was her *first* admission that *she* had *done* anything.

Despite these side issues, her attention moved quickly to the important matter. *'What happened?'*

His response was to hand her a letter. In giving it to her, he said, 'This will explain my connection with events at the Hazzard Laboratories.'

The letter was addressed to Military Liaison in Washington, D.C. It stated:

'We have on hand your cautionary reminder. Since I have been temporarily attached to this office for nearly six weeks now, I am with Major Porter's concurrence herewith answering on his behalf.

'The major and I have taken note of your statement that it is now more than two decades since the secret information, which became known as The Pentagon Papers, was leaked to *The New York Times*. We are determined not to be lulled by the fact that no comparable raid has been made on confidential material since that time. We welcome your admonishment to be careful. It is Major Porter's estimate that here in the west coast office there are thousands of documents relating to large and small industrial complexes, which manufacture equipment for the military and for the space programme under heavy security regulations.

'It is my belief,' the letter continued, 'that if the personal details that we have in our files were ever leaked to the media, the public would become highly critical of the moral rectitude of the top people in industry and science. Since I came here directly from a long tour abroad, particularly in the European theatre, I am in a position to report how startling some of this information has been to me. I am particularly surprised at the profound influence of the man-woman relationship on security matters. In Europe, the mixing of sex and war and espionage is a commonplace. To find it here in virtually equal intensity makes me wonder if perhaps America is not being Europeanized rather than the reverse.

'I feel that this first reaction I have is worth holding onto. It is so easy to become anaesthesized, so to speak, to human misbehaviour. And so, while I continue to have a keen awareness, I would like to send you some of the background aspects of the case I was brought over to solve. I propose in several letters, along with the appropriate tape transcriptions, to deal with one aspect at a time, and make comments on implications which seem important to me in my heightened reaction state. (Since this case is still unresolved, perhaps your experts might give us some suggestions.)

'As you know, when we move in on a company, large or small, we send in teams of technicians. These individuals not only check the organization's alarm and security system but they also bug the place thoroughly. The information from dozens of hidden microphones comes here to our computer, and is organized and cross-indexed. It is then available for study by authorized personnel.

'The aspect of the case which I am enclosing may be of particular interest to you because of the considerable publicity that attended the death (by a hit-run driver) of Dr. Carl Hazzard a year ago – if indeed he can be said to have died.

'You will observe, though the fact has not yet been reported to the public, that the disembodied brain of Dr. Hazzard is now mobile. At the request of the Brain Study Foundation, a special agent of the Motor Vehicle Department gave him a drivers' test.' He passed the test, and received his licence. If for any reason he is challenged by a traffic officer, he is to show a special card which, apparently, he is physically able to extend through the car window.

'At the moment, I have no comment about the so-called alienoids, but will have trusted (whatever that means these days) agents listen to the tapes, which minute-by-minute record the events taking place at the Hazzard Laboratories.

'Presumably, since leading members of the alienoid gang were briefly under arrest, there will be further developments. But it should be noted that –'

That was as far as her copy of the letter went. Marie looked up. 'Is there more?' she asked.

A strong, lean, tanned hand reached across the table, took hold of the sheets, and tugged them out of her fingers. Marie watched silently as Nicer folded the letter, and pushed it into an inside breast pocket.

'That's all you need to know, isn't it?' He spoke in a light tone.

'I'm breathless,' said Marie.

But she realized she was also relieved. She recognized special consideration when she saw it. And this that he was doing was a very intimate thing. Under other circumstances, it would have been extremely wrong of him to reveal to any top person of the Hazzard Laboratories that the place was under close surveillance.

– He must know *everything*, she thought.

As she considered the implications, the colour started up her cheeks. And yet, once again, the sense of relief came, stronger than before.

Philip Nicer said, 'I'm taking it for granted that you will not reveal the contents of that letter to anyone.'

'Of course,' said Marie. 'But now, quick tell me. Who attacked us, and what were they after?'

'They removed something in a truck,' he said cautiously. 'We don't know what yet.'

Marie stared at him across the table, momentarily blank. Then she put her fork down. Then: 'You can't be serious. You stopped them, didn't you? You arrested them all, surely?'

Even as she spoke the words, the realization was in her that he had done nothing of the kind.

'But why not?' Her voice was high-pitched. 'Why not?'

The man shook his head, with a faint smile. 'You've got

us confused with the police.' He explained matter-of-factly, 'They're not our kind of business.'

'B-but they're a gang of conspirators.'

Even as she uttered the protest, the truth was sinking in. 'You can't be serious,' she said. 'You let them all go.'

'They left –' he shrugged – 'and we didn't stop them.'

'B-but –'

The lean face was visibly amused now at her bewilderment. 'This country swarms with special interest groups that operate outside the law,' said Nicer, 'or at its precarious edge. We have now got this group recorded in our files, and we may gradually accumulate further information about the people in it.' He spread his hands in a dismissing gesture.

Marie was recovering, and beginning to have a glimmer of the limitations by which government agencies operated. She thought: – The left eye of the law does not pay attention to what the right eye is looking at . . .

It was a momentary glimpse of the espionage universe of Colonel Philip Nicer. For that moment, she was fascinated. The next instant, suspicion surged.

'Then it isn't over,' she said.

'I *hope* it is.'

Marie hesitated. She was reluctant to make an accusation; but the doubting thoughts had come. Abruptly, she couldn't stop herself. 'How,' she asked – the first question – 'did the alienoids find out where Carl was?'

Nicer chuckled softly. 'We had a woman call up police headquarters, and tip them off. We figured the information would be passed on. And it was.'

'B-but –' Marie began.

She couldn't go on. The large thought that was suddenly in her mind was that, not 'we', but he had done this. And that he had done it in order to put the pressure on a woman.

On her.

Her memory raced over the letter she had just read; recalled Nicer's suave reference to the mixing of sex, business, and espionage in Europe – implying that such things were done by *other* people. And that the behaviour involved was new in America.

– For God's sake, Marie thought, he's the worst of them all.

But she knew better. Not worst; merely the same. Men were like this. They moved in on a woman without mercy. And, presently, after she was captured she forgot exactly how it had been done. And, besides, there was also the ego satisfaction in being wanted.

Sitting there, she coined a Dr. Marie Hazzard aphorism about the man-woman thing: 'All human males are rats, but some of them are charming rats because they like *you* and not someone else.'

Even as she made up the pleasant little bit of wit – not an aphorism at all, not basic – her body, and the way she moved her head, *reflected* (if only the language could be read) that there were but a few types of males that she had ever even noticed: the Dr. MacKerries, the Dr. Hazzards, and the Colonel Philip Nicers. Other men – the kind who make good husbands – she had *never* noticed, as men. She looked through them as if they were neuter objects in space-time.

Unobservant of her tunnel vision in relation to males, slightly amused for a moment by her pleasant thought, Marie grew aware that Nicer was continuing his argument:

'My dear Marie,' he said, 'we absolutely have to find out what these alienoids are up to. So, last night we forced a confrontation.'

Marie remembered her second question. 'And who,' she asked, 'made the decision not to take these people into custody?'

There seemed to be no pause. Nicer said, 'I did.' His voice was steady, disarming.

On one level, that confirmed her swift suspicion. But on another, her own life experience reminded her that there were numberless problems that had no black or white solutions. It *was* possible that this particular group of criminals – the alienoids – should simply be taken note of by military intelligence agents.

Unfortunately, the practical result was that nothing was settled for sure. Nicer could guarantee only his implied belief that the alienoids were not a threat to national security. Meanwhile, his microphones and his men would continue to monitor Hazzard Laboratories, and she would be under his protection if anything developed.

That is, she would be if he accepted that a woman like her didn't have to pay the price, because – well –

Vague thoughts.

Which ended as, with a start, she remembered Carl. 'What about –' and there she paused, and then she used a word that had not crossed her lips in relation to Carl for nearly fourteen years – 'about my husband? Have you talked to him?'

And *he* did something instantly, also. 'Marie, think! This man Carl Hazzard –' Yes, *this man* was what he said – 'has shown an innate impulse to be a man of action. He has already of his own free will gone into extremely dangerous situations, and apparently handled himself skillfully in them. We must trust that he did the same last night.'

He glanced at his watch. 'We assumed the place might be mined, and of course we don't wish to be openly associated with what happened, so your watchman a few minutes from now – at 7:15 – will advise the F.B.I. of what happened. Now that it is light enough, they will go inside, and, conduct an investigation. We may assume that they will see to it that the phones are reconnected, and at that time you will have an opportunity to talk to Carl.'

Nicer concluded his formal summary: 'So far as Carl is concerned, our bugging system can only go by sounds and voices. All we heard from the Brain Room was the door open and men come in. No one said anything. No shot was fired. So our analysis is that Carl unlocked his door, and simply sat there pretending to be part of the equipment. Our guess is that he got away with it, because the men presently left.'

He glanced at her. 'Any comment?' he asked.

Marie said simply, 'Thank you. That's what I wanted to know.'

With that, the interflow between them warmed suddenly.

'What I would like,' said Nicer, 'is for this threat to continue – in view of the kind of woman you are – until . . . until . . .'

71

He stopped; and Marie finished for him: 'Until you're assigned to another theatre of action.'

It was, in fact, what he had started to say. But the truth was, this was his last assignment. He had put in for a release from duty by the end of the year. That was not a piece of information that he wanted known, as yet.

Nothing to do but attempt to recover. 'That's it,' he agreed. 'However –' more firmly – 'next time I phone you and ask if I can come up to visit you, that will be your moment of final decision. You can see that in my situation I cannot spend time in pursuit of a woman. What you decide next time will be yes or no forever.'

By that devious route, they were back on the kind of direct communication line that is possible between a man and a woman.

Marie flashed, 'Will you be faithful to me? I'd hate to be one of a harem.'

Nicer protested, 'I've only got twenty-four hours a day. I sleep about six. I'll call you four nights a week, and we'll meet here at this hotel. That room up there is a permanent room I maintain –'

'When? What hour?'

He told her, and she was startled. 'Are you serious? *That* late every time?'

'Every time,' Nicer echoed, with a faint smile.

The dialogue sounded intensely real to both of them; and they both showed slightly stronger colour in their faces. Under other circumstances, with someone other than Marie, the breakfast might have ended in a wild dash for the hotel room.

But the truth was he had already conveyed the wrong thought. She was to be a temporary girl friend, casually discardable on the day of his departure. On the surface, Marie ignored that reality. In many ways, she was sophisticated. Her observations of life told her that people did things like that. And so she talked glibly, as if next time – whenever that might be, now or later – she would not be a barrier.

This, alas, falsehood was not subjected to an immediate test. Nicer had been glancing at his watch again. 'I really

72

have to go,' he said reluctantly. 'I do have that 7:45 meeting.'

Outside in the street, as Nicer hailed a cab for her, Marie noticed the headline on a paper at the corner newsstand: 'HUGE VESSEL SIGHTED IN STRATO-SPHERE.' She said, 'I wonder what that could be.' Nicer bought the paper, but said nothing; simply held it so that she could see it more clearly.

She had time to read the first few lines: 'Astronaut Roger Dord, returning from a spacelab tour, reports sighting a large, cigar-shaped object in rapid motion –'

The cab door was open. Nicer guided her to it. As she stopped to climb in, she said, 'That's probably all we need: another flying saucer craze –'

Inside the cab, sitting, she thought: – Alienoids, flying saucers, ugh! . . .

Mrs. Gray let her in the front door. As she stepped across the threshold, the phone started to ring. 'Oh,' Marie was delighted, 'they've got it reconnected. Good.'

She hurried into her office-study and picked up the receiver, and said, 'This is Marie Hazzard.'

'Dr. Marie,' said a man's voice, 'this is Paul Gannott. Is my name familiar to you?'

'N-no.'

'Your husband didn't think it would be. So I'm sorry to have to inform you that in two outings that he made as a mobile unit, he mixed in matters that were none of his business. So last night we went into your laboratories and captured him –'

Marie was silent; blank. Something inside her was sinking, down, down. A sense that she was listening to someone who spoke out of a position of total power.

'Now, here is what you must do. Our big ship has arrived. It insists that it must take the disembodied brain of Dr. Carl back to Deea after the conquest of earth –'

Marie found her voice, but she really had nothing to say. 'I'm sorry –' she began, vaguely, 'I don't think I –'

Back to blankness.

The man's voice said, firmly, 'Dr. Marie, here is the situation so far as you are concerned. On its two previous

73

visits to earth, the ship was programmed to accept that earth wives accompanied their husbands wherever they went. We can deduce that a hundred years ago in the Victorian era when the first visit took place, the status of women was such that whoever did the programming took that for granted. What this means is that you must be completely ready to leave tomorrow night with all your baggage. Now, let's be sure you understand what to do. Have you got a pen or pencil handy?'

Suddenly, her mind was flying ... The important thing is to get that address – Belatedly, she remembered her phone recorder. Her fingers leaped and pressed the button. 'Yes, yes,' she murmured.

'The truck will come for you at nine o'clock,' said the baritone voice. 'If you wish we'll even take your furniture. We want you to be comfortable and happy. So be sure to take anything that you could possibly have any use for. Got that?'

'Yes,' mumbled Marie.

'That's all I have to say. Now, here's your husband to confirm what I've just told you.'

There was a pause. As Marie hesitated, Carl's unmistakable voice said in an eager tone, 'Marie, isn't this the greatest thing you've ever heard of?'

'Uh,' said Marie.

'Think, darling,' his voice went jubilantly, 'what this means for me. I've had no hope, just an endless blankness ahead of me living here with things that I know – the same old stereotype earth. Suddenly, the whole universe opens up. A race that has already conquered space travel. They're a little slow yet in their travelling, but they can put us both into periods of suspended animation six years at a time, and then six months of being conscious. Just you and me out there; and we fit together, Marie. Me, the sexual nothing, and you the forever good woman. Now, listen, dear, there's certain things that I'll need. Go into the Brain Room, and get –'

He named some of the recharge paraphernalia that was there, finished happily, 'Marie, out there in space I'll make up to you all my previous failures as a husband. We'll be such pals as no one has ever been before. I'm being signalled. Goodbye, for now sweetheart.'

'But,' said Marie, finally discovering her voice, and uttering the big thought that had been quivering all these moments at the tip of her tongue, 'what did Mr. Gannott mean, conquest of earth?'

'Oh, that,' said Carl, dismissingly. 'Being taken over by Deea simply means that Paul Gannott becomes sort of an ambassador-extraordinary with the power to interfere in all this nationalist nonsense that's going on on this planet, and put a stop to that finally and forever. There'll be a little trouble at first, but that doesn't mean anything. But even so, the safest place will be aboard the conquering ship. You see that, don't you? Okay, goodbye.'

There was the click of disconnection.

Chapter Nine

LOST PROTECTION

For Marie –

At the moment that she hung up, after the fantastic phone call, a mental mistiness descended on her. She stood; literally, she just stood, almost blank.

Vaguely, she was aware of the wonderful room: she called it her office-sitting room. Years ago, after the disaster to her marriage, she had surrounded herself with beautiful objects. The desk was a gleaming Italian antique of such breathtaking splendour that it lifted her spirit each time she looked at it, or even each time she glanced past it. The great, old, Italian effect was all around her: chairs that were worth thousands of dollars each, and a marvellous bureau for which she had paid nineteen thousand dollars of Carl's money. It had always given her a special pleasure to pay a lot for something: the look on Carl's face when he saw the bill was all by itself worth the price. Though he never actually said anything, he had once estimated aloud that her 'little' – the word was his; it wasn't exactly little – apartment, which consisted of the sitting room and the bedroom, had been furnished at an expense of more than three hundred thousand dollars.

As the vague recollection of that brought a tiny surge of the old pleasure, she was momentarily freed from fear. Abruptly, a thought. She grabbed the intercom phone. Several frantic moments later she was talking to the F.B.I. man who was temporarily monitoring the main gate. Through him she contacted the agent in charge of the investigation of the night-time attack.

The agent, whose name was Caulfield, came over to the house, a sturdy individual of about forty. He listened to the tape recording of her conversation with Paul Gannott and Carl. When it was finished, he looked at her helplessly.

'I really don't know what to make of that,' he said. He made a baffled gesture. 'This ship –' He stopped; and Marie jumped in verbally with an incoherent account of what she had read about a ship in the morning paper headline.

The F.B.I. agent waited politely for her to finish, then he said, 'I'll send somebody in here to make a tape copy of that conversation, and I'll relay it immediately to our headquarters in Washington. Locally, we'll check on Gannott.'

He broke off, 'By the way, the only things missing seem to be your, uh, husband's brain and that van your people tell me he was just starting to drive around in. Apparently, they loaded both him and it on a big truck, and drove off.'

The smallness of the damage seemed to reassure him, suddenly. His tone changed once more, became firm, 'Now, don't you worry. We'll have a welcoming committee here for anybody that comes by tomorrow night to pick up you and your luggage. But –' he shrugged, becoming matter-of-fact – 'the whole thing sounds to me like some kind of a practical joke.'

His was an unfortunate choice of a word. The one thing Marie was sure of was that what was happening was not a 'joke'. If Caulfield's purpose in describing it that way was intended to make her feel better, it failed miserably.

· The agent seemed not to realize his error, for he departed without any further attempt to reassure her. And there she was alone again. Marie sat down. And sat there. And sat. She kept swallowing. Mostly, she was blank. But periodically a rapid argument would go on inside her. In the argument she used the word, joke. As if by echoing it over and over it would take on meaning.

After each argument, blankness descended once more. It enveloped her mind like a mask without eyeholes or breathholes.

After a while, the phone rang. It was the F.B.I. man reporting that Paul Gannott, the banker, was neither at his office nor at his home address.

'I've advised Washington,' he said. 'But they don't know either what to make of this ship. Except for the report

77

from the astronaut, nobody has seen it. Which –' he added hastily – 'doesn't mean it isn't there. At those distances, you really have to know where things are, to spot them.'

Caulfield's voice as he spoke had a faraway, impersonal sound. He finished, 'I'll keep in touch.'

Plainly in her ears came the sound of his phone disconnecting; that startled her. She had intended to say something. A question in her mind was, exactly how did the F.B.I. propose to protect her the following night. She needed details. Suddenly, panic. She had the feeling that nobody was thinking about her. Or cared. Or was really interested.

Instantly, she had a strong impulse to call *both* Dr. MacKerrie *and* Philip Nicer. Her hands darted toward the phone. And then drew back.

The awful thought flickered that she had burned those bridges.

Resentment seethed . . . Damn those male rats! Doesn't a man ever have a human feeling for a woman? Is it all just sex? –

The rage ran its course; and she acknowledged within herself that both men were actually good-natured, and they even meant well in some obscure male fashion. In retrospect, she had an unhappy conviction that she had been extremely rude to Mac and tricky with Nicer.

But what can a woman do? she thought. There's always this pressure . . . At times she had the feeling that a man never had anything else on his mind.

It seemed to her finally, wearily, that what she had said to MacKerrie in breaking with him, *was* irrevocable. But that what she had said to Nicer had left the door open; and – well to remember – Nicer had given her a number to phone in case of need.

– Okay, she decided, I'll call and tell him I give in – in exchange for . . .

Pause. For what?

What could he do?

It was not a question, she realized presently, that she could afford to analyze. She needed somebody who had a personal interest in her. An individual who would not merely – like the F.B.I. agent – be around in a formal way. She craved an interest closer than that.

As that decision finally surged, she reached for and lifted the phone receiver.

There was a knock on the door. Mrs. Gray peered in. 'Dr. MacKerrie is here.'

Even as she spoke, the physician came into view beyond the housekeeper. 'Marie,' he called to her, 'I must talk to you.'

Marie replaced the receiver, and stood up. 'Thank you, Mrs. Gray. Come in Mac.'

She felt vague. The visit was a surprise; but not desperately so. MacKerrie was the genius who had salvaged Carl's brain from his destroyed body. For the most part he lived in one of the little cottages on the other side of the laboratory building.

As he came across the room toward her, it occurred to Marie, watching the deliberateness of his walk, that he was the perfect surgeon in his life as well as in the operating room. Not a single unnecessary motion. Every cut planned in advance.

It required several moments for her to shake off the effect of his ... automaticness (that was her term for it.) During those moments, MacKerrie reached her, and took her hand.

The action had its own reality.

This was a man and a woman who for whatever reason had had sex with each other. That knowledge would always be in their eyes if their glances met, or in their fingers or palms if they touched.

MacKerrie had not been one of those unfaithful male types who cause a woman to feel grief. Also, it was he who unmistakably wanted their intimacy to continue. So there was nothing that she could be mad about or take special offence at.

True, he *had* taken advantage of her. But it was not, and never had been, rape. She had resented him, but she had for her own reasons held still for what he did.

What had happened between them gave her the right now to reach over – which she did – and gently but firmly

79

remove his hand from her arm. And it gave him the awareness that her act was not a mortal insult.

Moreover, he had the experience of a man of forty who was also a doctor, who understood that her act of withdrawal was the kind of thing that women did. It was also real to him that a woman could be absolutely obnoxious to a man, and still at some later time accept him back. With that intent in mind, he parted his lips –

And the phone rang.

The sound broke the peculiar tension of this first meeting after her break with him. Relieved, Marie said, 'I'll be with you in a moment.'

She picked up the receiver and sat down in the magnificent desk chair. She gestured for MacKerrie to be seated, also. 'It's Walter,' she whispered. 'Long distance.'

The physician sat, and idly listened to her end of the conversation. The monologue was purely laboratory business, of no interest to him. And so MacKerrie was about to turn his attention back to his own thoughts – when he realized something: Marie's voice projected a husky richness.

He was instantly electrified, and stunned. It was to him, who had so much awareness, the voice of a woman who was sexually compatible with someone.

Marie's decision to surrender to Nicer was so swiftly perceivable by a trained observer. What was to her an unnoticed relaxing, and an unmonitored but immediate erotic stimulation, and more – it was all suddenly audible in her voice, in the way she held herself, and subtly many otherwises.

MacKerrie did not give Walter a thought in connection with Marie's radiant state. From the beginning, the pretense of the chief physicist (that he was also having an affair with Marie) was obvious to him. He understood it perfectly. He used it coolly to keep Marie off balance. At all times he had known full well that Walter was impotent, and that he (MacKerrie) had full possession of the woman.

The hormonic overtones of her voice were so unexpected that it overwhelmed him instantly – just as Marie hung up, and said, 'Walter has several important orders from a number of universities, but he'll be delayed in his return.' By the time those words were spoken, MacKerrie was trembling with an awful jealousy.

'Who is the man?' he half-yawned. 'Who are you dating?'

It was so abrupt, and unanticipated, that she could only gaze at him, all the while shrinking inside. Her thought of course immediately jumped to the possibility that he had spied on her the night before, and knew about Nicer.

After a moment, it struck her that there was really nothing to know. She began to recover. 'Are you out of your mind?' she said. 'There's been no one.'

If he heard her, it didn't seem to affect him. He was visibly in a state. Perspiration was on his forehead. Eyes were widened. Face was contorted. He leaned tensely forward.

Suddenly, it was apparent that he *had* heard. He leaned back. He sighed. Then muttered, 'What's going on? I tried to phone you this morning, and was told the phones were disconnected. What? –'

It was the opportunity to divert him from what he had, in his fashion, so accurately detected. Quickly, she summarized the events of the night. Then she played the tape of her phone conversation with Paul Gannott and Carl.

She was slightly startled to realize that his extreme jealousy had given her an odd sense of security. It was better (said that feeling) to have an insane personal interest from someone than to have none at all from anybody.

Consciously, she argued against the irrational reaction. But it remained with her all the while she watched him as he listened to the recording. What he had heard seemed to irritate him.

When the tape had been replayed, when all the words had been re-spoken once more, MacKerrie said impatiently, 'Marie, I really don't know what to do about Carl.'

In a frustrated voice, he described what Carl had confided in him about his two trips. MacKerrie continued, 'His foolishness in seeking out this dangerous group of wealthy cultists has jeopardized the Brain Foundation's costly experiment with him. As things stand, it looks as if I

81

made a mistake, also. I immobilized him to stop further hare-brained adventures, and that worked against him last night. Presumably, he might have escaped if I hadn't done that. Still, the alternative could be that he might have killed one or more persons. Then what? Would he be arrested, and tried for murder?' The surgeon shook his head angrily. 'Damn it, Carl assured me he had given them the slip; and since he is normally a cool-minded super-science type, I believed him. But he was evidently wrong.'

It scarcely seemed like the moment for Marie to explain that a Colonel Philip Nicer had given away Carl's identity and location. And that she believed Nicer had been motivated by a personal interest in her.

MacKerrie went on, 'My advice is, pay no attention to this so-called message. Don't prepare for a fictitious journey into space. Advise the police and the F.B.I., and let them take over.'

'I've already informed the F.B.I.' Swiftly, she summarized *that* information. Having given it, she expressed her Big Doubt. 'Why would Carl have talked the way he did?'

'For God's sake, Marie –' MacKerrie was impatient again – 'the poor guy is under pressure. There he is with these nuts, and he realizes he's got to play along with their delusion. Can't you see, he's fighting for time? And you know he always was one of the world's best actors.'

– Of course, thought Marie.

Pause. Then: 'What did you say this woman's name was, that Carl told you about?'

'Silver.'

The name, so unusual, seemed to fit the situation. With that, the utter madness of it all penetrated. And – just like that – she was grateful to MacKerrie.

The physician, who had been watching, waiting, hoping, saw the change in her. At once, he was on his feet, and over to her. 'Marie, my poor darling. What a strain this must be!'

It was one of those moments that no man will ever appreciate.

For MacKerrie, Marie's sudden relaxation signalled that

82

he could now lead her into the bedroom and they would engage in the sex act.

Such a thought did not even cross Marie's mind.

For her part, she was aware of his hand closing over hers. Aware of being drawn to her feet by his strength. Except, it wasn't quite like that. In that moment of relief and gratitude she parted her lips, and said urgently, 'Mac, you're the only one that can free Carl. You've got to go to Gannott's house, and somehow –'

She stopped, vague. But the feeling was that, as a man, he would know what to do.

There are words, and words, and words. The particular specimens that she had used penetrated MacKerrie's ears, and pinged into a part of his brain in a way that actually weakened him physically. His fingers, so strong moments before, became limp. He sort of let her go, and sort of drifted back away from her. And stood there helpless before her female mental machinery.

It was the male to-hell-with-it reaction to a woman when she was like this, that presently rescued him. MacKerrie braced that firm, well-exercised physician's body. He said, trying to make his voice matter-of-fact. 'I have to go now. I'll think about what to do for Carl, and this whole business, and call you later.'

Something in his tone brought Marie an awareness of his disappointment, and her first dim realization that maybe she understood what he wanted. She dismissed that partial insight instantly, because it was ridiculous. Mac was a gentleman. Obviously, he wouldn't expect a woman like her in broad daylight, with all the daylight possibilities of interruption –

MacKerrie was turning toward the door. 'I'll call you later,' he said in an almost formal tone.

'B-but –' began Marie, startled.

The physician seemed not to hear. And moments later the corridor door had opened and closed. And he was gone.

Marie stood rigid. Inside her was an emotional dilemma, unsolvable. There was a need to have MacKerrie around without paying the price, and the simultaneous need to send him to rescue Carl – or at least do *something*.

83

'B-but –' she echoed now, blankly.

Silence answered.

It was not clear what had happened. MacKerrie's yelling had done something negative. The feeling of willingness to surrender to Nicer had turned off.

And of the personal interest that she had craved so desperately – and which MacKerrie's presence had seemed to represent, and which Nicer's attitude seemed to promise – there was not a shred now perceivable.

A stunned Marie actually went into her bedroom, and slept for a while.

Chapter Ten

THE SLEELE STRIKES

Earlier.

After Marie's taxi drove off, Colonel Philip Nicer walked to a cab that was parked a short distance down the street. He got in with only a greeting to the driver. The man seemed to know what he wanted and who he was. He started his machine in motion immediately.

At first, no words were exchanged. The driver, a young man in his twenties, kept his attention on the traffic and the street. Nicer sat like a passenger in the rear seat, with a faint frown on his face reading the news account of the large spaceship, the presence of which had been reported by the human astronaut.

Finally, he nodded, folded the paper, let it drop on his lap, and said, 'Anything you wish to say or report?'

The conversation that resulted from that question in a way meant what it said, and in another way didn't. It was designed to take account of, of all things, passing mind readers.

'Only a question. What do you think the Deeans are up to?'

'Another ship has come,' said Nicer. 'Their third in a hundred years.'

'Do we care?'

'Not basically.'

'Suppose this time it's conquest?'

'It probably is a combination,' said Nicer thoughtfully. 'The mathematics of it goes something like this. Each ship is about fifty years *en route*. So the first one left Deea one hundred and fifty years ago. The second was dispatched when the first was arriving in the solar system. However, this third one was probably not sent until the first actually returned to Deea with the information that the initial landing had taken place, and that the several thousand embryos it carried here had been successfully transformed by the Luind method into human males, and safely landed, and hidden in private orphanages. With that information, they could decide on conquest as being feasible for this trip.'

He shook his head regretfully. 'Too bad. We Luinds are trying by our devious methods to civilize these various aggressive races. We gave them all, to begin with, our method of converting one life form into any other at the embryo level. That enables the new arrivals to mingle unseen and unsuspected. It also often has a psychological effect on the transformed embryos when they reach adulthood. But most important – and that was our purpose in releasing the technique – it has definitely influenced them to send in an advance force to infiltrate the prospective victim planet.'

'From what I learned at the secret Luind School,' ventured the cabman, 'they've all had unpleasant surprises when somebody turned out to be more powerful than the aggressors anticipated. What do you think of the human race? Do you think they'll be able to use the hydrogen bomb against a Deea takeover?'

'No, they don't have good enough missiles.'

'Too bad.' The youthful driver seemed concerned. 'I sort of like it here, and since of course I have to be a human being all my life, I feel personally affected.'

Philip Nicer shrugged. 'I also have to be human. But the fact is, our appearance is not held against us when we return to Luind.'

'Still – the female situation . . .'

'We're allowed to take a human woman,' smiled Nicer. 'In fact, when my father arranged to appear to die, so that I could legally inherit, he took my mother with him. Last word I had she's happy.'

'Your father must be smarter than I am,' said the cabman. 'I can't seem to figure out the human female.'

'Well –' Suddenly, Nicer was frowning – 'they do seem to be an unusually complex type. Still, as a result we all bring male embryos only. The assumption is that we'll be motivated as individuals to mingle, and to try to understand human psychology. If we had our own females, we'd be tempted to remain an in-group. As it is, we have to learn what it takes to get a human woman, and no fooling.'

'What do you think Metnov will do?'

'That's one of the things I'll find out when I meet his and Gannott's agent this morning. Apparently, Gannott has already informed Metnov about this spaceship – evidently fears him more than he does us. Notice, we're advised *after* the ship arrives. I plan to say that we have no instructions to defend earth, even though we could use the planet against Metnov's people at a future time.'

'None of the other alien groups here care?'

'None.'

The driver was silent for a block; then: 'You've always said that the real question at a time like this has to do with relationships of key persons with human women.'

'True.' A fleeting image of Marie passed before Nicer's mind's eye. He leaned back in the seat.

'What about that blonde bombshell Paul Gannott married?'

'Well –' with a faint smile – 'the solution-system I used there *was* my one attempt to interfere in this matter. But it doesn't seem to have worked.'

'What was the theory behind that?'

'What you said.' Nicer laughed curtly. 'Give a man what he thinks he wants in a woman. Then later check to see if he and she in their automatic fashion demolished each other. Gannott, apparently, could not be demolished in that fashion.'

Oddly, every word uttered by the two men was true in its fashion. But the dialogue also had the meaning that the Luinds were opposed to the Deean takeover, though they would do nothing overt to stop it. They would, however, dabble in an intricate, roundabout, reasoning resistance which, handled right, could make unpleasant waves for the aggressors and might even cause cyclones, so to say.

No additional remarks were made. The taxi arrived at a long, low structure. The sign over the building read: LOST SOULS   Cocktail Lounge and Restaurant   Open 24 Hours.

The cab turned into the driveway, and stopped short of the entrance near the first parking lot. The driver said, 'Shall I park in the usual place?'

'Yes.'

Nicer did not leave the taxi immediately. It looked like an ordinary yellow cab, but it was actually an armoured vehicle. From the comparative safety inside, he looked out, searching for any spot from which a high-powered rifle might be used against him.

Like so many buildings on the north side of the 'strip', the Lost Souls bar and this lot had been built into the side of a hill. And so there was a steep embankment which, at this early hour, offered a vista of concrete and dirt, with scrub brush higher up.

A man climbed out of one of the other cars parked nearby, and walked over to Nicer's machine. Nicer lowered his window an inch. 'Hello, Captain,' he said.

The man, who was not in uniform, said, 'We've got three operatives up there, covering the lot.'

Nicer wanted to know who they were.

Captain Bendley hesitated, then excused himself and went off. He spoke to someone in another of the parked cars. When he returned to Nicer's car, he named three names in a low voice.

Nicer said, 'Just a minute.'

He leaned back and remembered the men by his method. Presently, he nodded.

With that he opened the door, climbed out, and waved to the cab driver. The taxi drove off, and Nicer glanced at Captain Bendley, who said, 'We've got four of our men inside the bar.' With a smile he named them – and waited for Nicer's reaction.

Nicer had one of the four, a swarthy man named Emile McGordon, called outside. McGordon had a Latin look, despite his Scotch or Irish name, and he had been assigned by Major Porter and was not a Luind. Out of the way was the best place for him.

A minute later, having taken all the precautions he could think of, Nicer entered the Lost Souls Cocktail bar. The time was exactly 7.45 a.m.

Nicer entered the bar by way of the parking lot entrance. As he came in, he searched for and found the door to the street.

In a series of quick glances, then, he took in the long L-shaped room with its leather-covered booths set against the walls. The booths had high sides. A couple in one of them could be almost out of sight.

Nicer walked past each booth, noticed where the restrooms were, and mentally marked an arrow sign indicating the location of the phone booths.

At the entrance to the restaurant section, he made his longest pause; let his eyes become accustomed to the shaded lights; surveyed the dim interior.

Satisfied, he concentrated again on the bar. Like the restaurant, it also was half full, which seemed a normal quota of 'lost souls' at this hour for a place like this.

In his speedy examination, Nicer had noticed several familiar persons, all Intelligence agents, and all, of course, on such an occasion, also Luinds like himself. One of the other officers – Jameston – caught his eye and indicated a man sitting on a stool at the bar.

Nicer walked over and settled beside the man. 'Mr. Griffen?' he asked.

The man turned. 'Hey,' he said, 'you're Nicer.'

He was about forty, with a face that was more round than lean, not exactly ugly, but his nose was slightly pug, his lips a little too thick, his skin showed wrinkles.

'Maybe you can help me make up my mind,' he asked. 'Joanie wants to marry me.' He held out his hand. 'By the way, my full name is Abraham – you know, after the biblical character, Abraham – Abe Griffen.'

Nicer ignored the extended palm, and it presently withdrew.

'Women,' Abe continued, 'have a lot to explain.'

Nicer stared at the man. Since Abe was a Sleele, his remarks had to be misleading. As it was, if he remembered the purpose of this meeting it didn't seem as important to him as his concern over Joanie.

'I used to think,' Abe went on, 'that women on earth were next to angels. You know: God, Christ, the Holy Ghost,

Disciples, Angels, Women – then maybe came flowers and trees and some of the domestic animals, and finally, practically at the bottom, men. But now I'm not so sure.'

Nicer had recovered. It seemed to him that although the conversation was on an important subject, it had moved away from him too quickly.

He said, 'Before we get off on men's favourite topic, you know what we're here for?'

'Oh, yeah, sure,' Abe said. He reached into his pocket, drew out a sealed envelope, and held it out to Nicer. Nicer gazed at it distastefully, and said finally, 'Now, come on, Abe, you know it would be foolish of me to open a letter from Metnov.'

Abe was surprised. 'If anything happened to you, I might be hurt, too. And you know he wouldn't do that to me. I'm his brother.'

'All Sleeles are brothers,' said Nicer. 'But some of them have been killed in operations planned by Metnov. So – why don't I just slip off this stool and step over behind that pillar. Then you open the letter, and read it to me in a loud, clear voice.'

He didn't wait for acceptance, but hastily got to his feet and walked over behind the sturdy looking pillar. He stood there, then, as Abe's voice read out the message from Metnov:

Dear Phil: Paul Gannott called me yesterday through my Paris relay, and asked me if I would tell you that earth was about to be the recipient of a glorious gift. It was going to be permitted – he said – to become a colony of Deea. He promised that casualties would be limited to those persons who resisted, and that in no way would the takeover ever be used as a means of barring you and me and our associates from operating on earth and in the solar system. If you could ever bring yourself to overcome your distrust of me, we might one of these weeks get together and discuss the implications for the Sleele brotherhood and the Luind peoples of such a takeover. Failing that, you may ask questions of my brother, Abe, and he is authorized to reply to the best of his ability. Helen sends her love.

Sincerely,

Metnov

'That's it,' said Abe.

'Thanks,' Nicer called, 'now place it back in the envelope, and slip it into your right back pocket. I'm going to sit on the stool to your left.'

Moments later, having been assured that the envelope and its letter were indeed in the designated pocket, Nicer did just that.

'You look,' Abe greeted him, 'like somebody who understands human women.'

'Not me,' said Nicer, remembering Marie with a rueful smile.

'I guess,' Abe was saying, 'I got the wrong idea about girls because I started chasing after them so young. By the time I was seventeen, boy, I was going at it regular. But each one of those females made such a big deal out of sex that, in spite of the indoctrination I was getting telling me that I wasn't really human, I was a Sleele, they got me to feeling sinful. You may not believe this but I cut the stuff out three times before I was twenty-one, just out of guilt. But what I want to know now is, if they're so damn pure how come I got so many of them?'

He paused and gazed at Nicer as if expecting an answer. When none came, he went on, 'Joanie wants to marry me. I say she should give up the others and then maybe I'll think about it.'

Nicer interjected, 'What others?'

Abe seemed not to hear. 'Joan says no. It took her a long time to get these fellows to like her, and she's had bad experiences in giving up friends in order to get married. Then the man didn't marry her after all, she says. So, she says, the day we get the licence she'll call up these men and give some story about having to go out of town. So then if we marry within a week, she'll call them up and cancel them out, she says. But if we don't get married – if I chicken out like the others did in the past –'

Nicer said, 'Why not find yourself a woman who hasn't got all those other entanglements?'

Abe stared at him as if it were a new idea. Then he shook his head. 'Joanie's the one that appeals to me,' he said in a helpless tone.

'How many men has she got?'

'Six – including me.' He was abruptly cheerful. 'I get the extra day each week.'

'Well –' said Nicer, doubtfully.

Abe interjected, 'If I chicken out, Joanie says, then she'll just pick up where she left off, except that I won't be in the circuit anymore. She says she couldn't stand me to be around once I had promised to marry her and didn't. I haven't promised yet, so I can keep going like I am.'

Nicer knew of several arrangements whereby an earth woman, by one means of another, maintained a harem of males. In Joan's situation no money seemed to be involved, and Joanie had a hard time holding the men. So her system had a flaw in it.

Still, the method she had was somehow keeping this Sleele brainwashed. Might be worth looking into, and was definitely to be encouraged.

Abe persisted, 'Well, what do you think?'

Nicer asked, 'Has Joan ever been married?'

'No.'

'Well –' Nicer spoke expansively – 'then I think you should marry her. Every woman ought to be married at least once in her life.'

Abe slipped off his stool eagerly. Then his expression clouded, and he sat down again.

He said soberly, 'I was going to go and tell her, but the particular guy who has Thursday night gets to stay until nine a.m. I'll have to wait until then before I give her the happy news. How about another drink?'

Nicer accepted the cocktail thoughtfully. 'Does Joanie work?'

'From noon until six,' nodded Abe. He raised his glass. 'Here's to marriage,' he said.

'No,' said Nicer. He raised his glass. 'I'm getting a new thought here – I don't know why I didn't notice it before. Here –' he touched glasses – 'here's to earth women.'

'Hey,' said Abe, 'I'll drink to that.'

After they had sipped, Nicer said, 'And now, one question: where are the Deeans operating from? Where's the headquarters?'

Abe Griffen hesitated. 'Oh,' he said finally, 'that. Boy, you got a one-track mind.' He shrugged. 'Well, they moved that computer from the Hodder house to Gannott's place.'

'That estate of his at the south end of town?'

'Yep.'

'Jolson Road?'

'Right.'

'How can I get in touch with Metnov if I need him fast?'

'Call his Paris relay.'

'How can I get in touch with you?'

The other man drew out a card. 'Here's Joanie's number.' He held the card to Nicer, but the latter smilingly shook his head, and instead, got out his notebook and copied the information from the card while Abe held it. When the job was done, Abe slipped the card back into his pocket. 'You're a suspicious guy,' he said.

'This is a hard world,' said Nicer. 'What looks like paper can be synchronized with one person – say, you – but will burn off the fingers of anyone else who touches it. I want to keep my fingers so I can shake Metnov's hand if we ever meet.'

'Shake mine,' said Abe. He held it out.

Nicer climbed warily off his stool, backed off, and shook his head. 'I hate to be discourteous,' he said, 'but there's a type of energy that you can, so to speak, palm off on someone else, and it doesn't affect him until a few minutes later. Good luck with Joanie.'

As Nicer turned away, Abe called, 'I don't have the feeling this conversation is over.' Nicer paused and faced the man at a respectful distance. 'It is well known,' he said, 'that at a couple of hundred feet Sleeles can read minds.'

'What we Sleeles know,' said Abe, 'is that a Luind can be talking and apparently thinking on one subject, and actually mean something different.'

'Now, now Abe,' Nicer chided, 'don't project that Sleele tendency to be devious on the rest of us.'

'Metnov,' said Abe, 'keeps having the feeling that in a crisis like this we'll be used by the Luinds to solve the problem. And we won't even know how it was done.'

'That,' said Nicer, 'has got to be the Sleele temperament

combined with the human body-brain tendency to have paranoid fantasies. We Luinds were surprised by the arrival of the Deean ship.'

'It's Metnov's delusion,' said the other, 'that Luinds are never surprised. Their problem is that they have to accomplish their goal without any real support from their home planet.'

'If only,' said Nicer, 'we were so prescient as never to be surprised.'

'We Sleeles,' came the reply, 'have the impression that after the Luinds use us to solve this problem, we won't be able to guess how they did it.'

'Luinds over-reach themselves sometimes just like Sleeles,' said Nicer.

'I suppose,' gloomed Abe, 'there's a clue in that very remark. But even though, according to you, I can read your mind, I can't see what that clue is.' When Nicer made no additional comment, Abe continued, 'What you gonna do about Gannott?'

'We don't have anything within a year's flight that could handle the firepower of Gannott's big ship. So we accept his peace offer. But –' grimly – 'we'll bring our battleship over if he goes back on his word. Tell him that.'

'I'll tell him,' said Abe, 'but Metnov won't believe it. He thinks you can have one of your big ones here in a couple of hours by your jump system. And the real big question is, why don't the Luinds defend all these single planet civilizations when they're attacked?'

'Granting,' said Nicer, 'that such a rapid jump transit exists – which I've never seen myself; and I keep wondering about the source of Metnov's information; I say, granting that, bringing such a super-ship here would be just what Metnov would like to have happen. Then he could see one in action; and smart Sleele scientists operating from key stations in the solar system might be able to figure out from its energy field what the method was. How about that?'

'What is all this secrecy about rapid space flight?' asked Abe. 'Why not give the method to everybody?'

'If I were to grant,' said Nicer, 'that such a method

existed, I might reason that some of the still-aggressive space powers like the Sleeles and the Deeans are taking control of remote planetary groups so long in advance because, when they get rapid flight, then they'll already have bits and pieces of an interstellar empire waiting for them.'

'All we Sleeles are interested in,' said Abe, 'are earth women. Look at Metnov – that Russian beauty, Helen, is just about driving him out of his mind; she keeps not wanting to tolerate those other females he keeps going after.' Abe shrugged. 'I solved all that by seeking out a woman who had other men. That way I taught myself not to be jealous.'

With that, he headed rapidly for the door; and Nicer went as quickly over to Jameston. 'When a Sleele first holds you with a set of delaying questions, and then leaves in haste, he may think he's accomplished something. What does the computer show?'

The slender man was studying the tiny TV set on his wrist. 'It's coming over now.' Pause, then grimly, 'He flicked his finger the last time he offered to shake your hand, and threw something in your face.'

Nicer reached the bar in two strides, grabbed his glass of water, and whipped it up to his face. Swiftly wiped it off with a napkin. Then more water, more wiping.

'Those Sleeles,' he said, with a strained smile, 'and that Metnov –'

He stopped. He fell to the floor like a collapsed sack. Or rather, he would have fallen except that Jameston grabbed at him. And another man leaped forward, and was somehow very quick about it. The two men held Nicer from crashing out of control, and presently carried him out of the bar and lifted him into the back seat of one of the parked cars. Bendley came over.

'I got your message,' he said, 'and we're holding the Sleele.' He pointed to where several agents had Abe in handcuffs. 'What happened?'

'A new drug? A new poision?' said Jameston. He beckoned to the men who held Abe. 'Bring him closer.'

And when the faintly smiling Abe had been brought

over, Jameston said grimly, 'If he's dead, this is one time we'll break our rule against retaliation.'

'He's not dead,' was the cool reply. 'After all, murder could endanger me. Metnov merely wants Nicer out of the way during the next few days. Take him home to bed, give him intravenous feeding. He'll wake up in four days.'

'You'll be around,' said Jameston. 'We're not as sold as you seem to be on Metnov's brotherly spirit.'

'I'm grateful to Nicer,' said Abe. 'He gave me some good advice about my girl friend; and I trust a Luind on things like that more than a Sleele. Metnov says to drop Joanie, but Nicer said I should marry her. So –' he concluded – 'a few minutes after nine I'd like to phone her and propose to her. Okay?'

'Okay,' said Jameston.

Chapter Eleven

A SECRET ENTRANCE OPENS

Carl was in a room, which he identified without difficulty as the library in a large home.

He had been brought to this – for him in his immobile state – prison in the wee hours, and left with a guard. And then after a while Paul Gannott came in. The two men – the alienoid from Deea and the bodiless brain of what had been a human being – had a conversation, mostly lies on Carl's part. But there had been that automatic growing interest in Gannott's purpose with him. The very first mention of the fifty year voyage with Marie as his companion, did something. His mind seemed to float free of all the tensions of the past year. Some part of him recognized the total irrationality of his reaction. But the excitement over-rode good sense.

The early morning phone call to Marie took place while he was in the over-stimulated condition. Then Paul Gannott departed. And once more only he and the guard remained.

Carl suppressed a strong impulse to test immediately what he could still do with his equipment. His cautioning thought to himself was: wait! Maybe these people could detect anything electronic he did. And were hoping that he would try something, so they could cut him off now, at once, from even those minor abilities.

He waited.

From where he had been wheeled, he could see a stretch of carpeted floor. Could see all three of the walls that had the book shelves right up to the ceiling. Could see the other wall, which was panelled, and chairs, two gleaming desks, settees, lamps, and the single long window. Unfortunately, the window was at the far end of the panelled wall, so he couldn't look outside. But he could see by the way the light came through it that it was daylight. In fact, he could even determine by the slant of the sunlight when it was noon and when mid-afternoon, and so on until finally there was twilight dimness. And night.

During that passage of time, the guard was changed every four hours. They were always men, well-dressed, educated, and capable-looking; and they, each in turn, found a comfortable location on a settee, and settled down with a book, glancing up occasionally at Carl.

The day was that uneventful. But he had had many such in the twelve months since his disaster; and he was resigned.

He kept recalling the immediate past. He had a memory of being taken from the blank interior of a truck into a large house. There was not much to see. The vehicle had been backed up close to a door, and so he had had only a glimpse of a tree-lined driveway as he was eased down a ramp. Views of hallways, several of them, all quite long, came later, suggesting that the house was large indeed.

Carl had his own internal time system, so he needed no window light to inform him of the time of night or day. But, nevertheless, it was seeing how dark it was outside that finally stimulated a decision.

He should know his situation. He should test.

At once, he activated what was potentially his only contact with Marie.

Marie had offered no objection to having a one-way TV-radio connection to what had once been his apartment in the house. 'It will be a familiar thing for me to look at,' he had said to her, 'whenever I feel depressed.'

At the time that he had conned her into acquiescing to that, his sly thought had been to sort of get one eye and one ear into the place. Eventually he hoped she would let him expand his connection.

That part hadn't worked out too well. 'Thank you, no –' Marie had said coldly, when he had suggested that a TV eye be put into her living room wall, also. And, when he had become mobile a few days before, she had made it equally clear that she would not welcome visits from him.

What she had allowed him was one-way in the sense that

he could see and hear what went on in the part of the house that had formerly been his living quarters. However, he couldn't talk *to* anyone who might be there.

It was this limited connection that Carl now tried to activate. To his somewhat excessive delight, the view came through instantly.

The first impression was of a deserted room. There was the familiar furniture: the bed perpetually made, the gleaming expensive desk, and a partially visible big chair to the left and half a clothes closet door to the right ... was the limit of his vision. Faint sounds came through the wall of the residence from the street: three cars went by and two motorcycles. Except for that, silence: the silence of a night city and of an unoccupied house.

Frustrating. He could watch and hear, but he could not speak. Nor could he project an image of himself or of where he was. Theoretically, it would be possible for an observant Marie to notice that the equipment was on. At which time, the two of them as capable physicists could undoubtedly work out a method of two-way communication. Unfortunately, the chance of Marie entering this part of the house was remote. Still –

Carl's thought was: – I'll make my other test. And just switch back here for the next twenty-four hours, in case she does come and does observe. (The other test had to do with control of the van.)

He was about to disconnect when – a sound. A door opened out of his line of vision. Moments later, Marie in her pyjamas and robe came into view. Her expression – what the startled Carl could see of it – was intent, even grim. She walked out of his sight. He heard a drawer open – and shut. Then she came in view again. Now she was carrying a small, red, leather-covered book. She walked past. And once again the door opened and shut.

The instantly bemused Carl had recognized the volume. It was his unpublished, bound manuscript of *Women Are Doomed: the Aphorisms of Dr. Carl Hazzard.*

– For God's sake, thought Carl. Marie! Interested in *that.*

Before his accident she had refused even to hold the

99

book in her hands. And had always immediately left the room when he started to quote from it.

Suddenly, thinking about that, it was a bad moment . . . If she's interested in what I have to say about the man-woman thing, it must be because –

Because why?

It seemed to the abruptly suspicious Carl that some male was on her mind. And she wanted to understand the truth of the matter. And, in her need, was willing to consider possibilities even from the abhorred Carl Hazzard.

Suddenly, his mind swam with fantasies of Marie being made love to by other men. So many of them that the very number of imagined lovers finally brought a return of calm. At which time he reminded himself that, really, it was none of his business what Marie did . . . after the way he had treated her. But he also remembered that after all Marie *was* the good-woman type described in his book. And that it was a sad scientist who did not accept his own systematic thought.

– And, he argued with himself, nothing has happened except maybe that business with Walter Drexel that could have put sufficient pressure on Marie to break her out of that particular uncriticisable position . . .

His thought in that moment of rationality was *that* close to the truth. Thus, he missed the disaster he had caused because he could not grasp what a fantastic pressure it had been on everyone involved.

His attention drifted. What bothered him was that Marie might return to replace the book. Therefore, he mustn't disconnect. The second test (with the van) accordingly would have to wait.

Ten minutes and twenty-three seconds went by according to the exact clock inside him. He had already had time to think wearily: – Okay, so I'm going to stay connected here until I'm sure she's asleep. Some time around midnight. And then . . .

The thought suffered a pregnant pause. For there was a sound.

Different.

– *The secret entrance!* He was instantly excited. He had

100

had the special door and hallway constructed during one of the times Marie was visiting her parents. So Marie never did find out how his mistresses reached his bedroom, or even that they came there at all.

Carl, watching electrified from a distance, had no doubt who *this* mistress must be. At this hour.

Silver.

As he waited, a beautiful young woman with long platinum tresses entered from behind a screen. She stood looking around uncertainly. Then spoke softly, 'Carl, are you there?'

He had never seen her before. That had been her stipulation: the room must be dark. But the wonderful voice – unmistakable.

Viewed now for the first time, she was fabulously good-looking.

Suddenly, Carl was shaken. It was not the first time, of course, but . . . This is what I lost – What she and he had done was one more of an incredible number of infidelities against Marie. Yet seeing Silver now for the first time, for the very first time, somehow brought a keener awareness of the disaster he had suffered a year ago. At that moment if he had had eyes tears would have flowed.

As Carl watched, helpless to say, or do, or interfere, the woman walked hurriedly to the door of the library-office that made up the second principal part of his apartment. For at least a minute she gazed inside. And obviously there was no one there, for she was visibly indecisive. Finally, a little uncertain, she came back past the eye of the camera through which Carl was watching, and headed out of his line of sight in the same direction as Marie had gone nearly fifteen minutes earlier. The same sound came of a door opening and shutting.

Carl thought, startled: – Good God, she's gone to talk to Marie . . .

Silence – that lengthened. He kept thinking that, surely, she would presently return this way.

But she didn't.

101

Chapter Twelve

EMERGENCE OF THE SHADOW SHIP

The main shock was over and accepted.

Marie sat in her marvellous bed, propped up by pillows. Her face felt flushed, and body tense. Carl's vicious little book, *Women Are Doomed*, lay open on her lap.

A sudden memory about one of the aphorisms had prompted her to go into what had formerly been his apartment. There, she had dug down into a certain drawer, where, a year before, she had first located the unpublished but neatly bound volume. Lips pursed now, she glared down at the item she had looked up:

'A large part of a woman's brainwashing (Carl had written) includes a set of assumptions that men do the risky things that have to be done in this world. In a woman's mind it is proper that men face garage mechanics, phone complaint departments, face bayonets, and shoot criminals. These unconscious assumptions lead automatically to a thousand lesser male-female relations, particularly those having to do with protection, security, and being cared for in emergencies. So long as a woman, or women, permit such attitudes to control them, she will deliver sex as payment and never as a gift. And both parties will accept that the price is right.'

It was such an exact description of what she had done with MacKerrie, that Marie had to agree: – Okay, that's where I am . . . And, furthermore, that was what she had intended to do with Nicer. She had desperately needed a couple of male lions – or at least (she corrected herself) she had thought she did, and, in the case of MacKerrie, thought she had. Instead, her phone call to Nicer had brought the startling response that he would not be available for several days. And her calls to the brave surgeon had all through the day triggered a tape answering system.

Marie grew aware that she was bracing herself. That her lips were pressed together. And her feeling was that it was time to make her final, once-and-for-all stand against such ideas.

Her thought: – All these years I've been trying to do what's fair and just. Trying to be – how was it Carl defined it in this damned little book of his on women? – in an uncriticisable position ... Which really meant, striving to live a faultless life. (And what, please, was wrong with that?)

Yet everything had gone wrong.

The first dim realization of how she had contributed to that wrongness was finally penetrating. But her new understanding did not absolve the male. In fact, more and more he was visible as the villain. After all, there was a difference between a naive and trusting person (the woman) and the swindler (the man) who took advantage of that trust.

The solution which now began to surface inside her was not an objective, scientifically thought-out thought. Indeed, its principle ingredient was outrage – which she observed but considered an appropriate emotion. And so, what came into view was actually another Great Big Automatic Process as unnoticed for what it was as the earlier naivete. To Marie it had the look of, at last, rationality.

The thought implicit in that process was: – By God, if that's the way the world is, if a person can spend an entire lifetime trying to do the right thing; and the first consequence is that she marries a Carl Hazzard; and the second consequence is that she has no normal life; and the third is that she is suddenly in danger of being falsely accused by that self-same Carl Hazzard of having participated in his murder; and in order to avoid *that* she has to permit herself to be, in effect, raped three times a week by Dr. MacKerrie. And then –

Because that same Carl never stopped causing trouble, suddenly this same woman had to have the protection of Colonel Philip Nicer; and in exchange therefore she was expected to provide *him* with sex four times a week; or else *he* wouldn't protect her –

Pause.

First decision: – Okay, life, you're a villain and not worth the paper you're printed on for a woman; so –

Inversion:

– Therefore, it doesn't matter anymore what happens to me . . . At the visceral level, that was the feeling-thought.

Final conclusion: – I will take all necessary risks (so help me) so that I shall never again be at the mercy of a man . . . regardless of consequences.

It was the famous decision, the implications of which have always been unnoticed by the maker. When made by a male, it creates that strange, intense being, the Real Man. And, when made by a female . . . has to be seen in action to be believed. Fantastic is often the only word for the consequent behaviour of a woman who has hitherto been in an uncriticisable position.

In this instance, Marie being who she was, the melodramatic decision, given a chance, might have presently been re-examined, and smiled out of existence. But at that precise moment, Marie heard a sound.

She looked up, startled.

A woman stood in her bedroom doorway. She had platinum blonde hair that streamed down past her shoulders, past her breasts. Her face, enframed in that almost silvery cascade, was the face of an angel. She was quite tall, almost five feet eight inches – taller than Marie by about two inches.

She said in a thrillingly musical voice, 'Carl is not in his room – again. I can't delay any longer. I had to come in and talk to somebody here. Don't be afraid.'

That last was spoken quickly, as Marie reached down with a convulsive gesture, and picked up the gas capsule discharger which she always had by her bedside as a protection.

'I'm not afraid,' said Marie, lioness. 'Who are you?'

'*Silver.*'

Pause. Silence. An of-course-I-should-have-known-feeling. And something else: enough shock to shut off certain reasoning portions of her brain.

The marvellous voice trilled, 'Dr. Marie, the ship is

here. Tonight, we can still do something. You must come with me – unless we can locate Carl at once. You're a scientist. I'll show you where and what. I –'

Marie heard none of these words. And so, at that point she shot the apparition in the doorway with the gas capsule discharger.

'Oh, my God,' said Silver, 'you shouldn't have done that.' She began to sag, to crumple. From the floor, moments later, she moaned, 'The two of us together might have – might have –'

Marie did not hear those words either in any real meaning of hearing. Oh, the sounds went into her ears. And they registered somewhere inside her brain. But the communication came to one of those dead ends that people have inside them. And vanished.

She got up. As she dressed, she recalled vaguely that Carl had once given her a pistol. But she had long ago carefully mislaid it. Pistols killed. Whereas her trusty little gas capsule discharger merely anesthesized.

Clutching the discharger in one hand, she walked over to the unconscious woman.

And stood there looking down at her.

Marie thought: – There's really a kind of satisfaction hitting, in effect – the gas gun hit its victim with a capsule that penetrated the skin – a woman who had cuckolded you. If that was the right term for it.

She was momentarily distracted. Was there a word for it when it was done to a wife? Or was the meaning of cuckolding entirely a derivative of the almost endless ages of male dominance?

Swiftly – because the gas soon lost its power – she put that out of her mind. Somewhat more slowly, she dragged the inert body through the kitchen and out of the side door into the garage. The night out there was blessedly pitch. But, since she did need a little bit of light to start, she went back and opened the kitchen door a crack. With that she could see her problem. But the actual strength required to drag Silver onto the floor of the rear seat was almost too much for Marie.

For a long while after the task was done, she stood

beside the open door of the car literally gasping for breath, and half leaning against the side of the car. Because of this accident of position, and the enforced (but otherwise peaceful) unmoving wait, she now had her first good look at Silver. In fact, she couldn't stop herself. There, directly beneath her eyes, was the platinum hair and the wonderful face.

After a while the beauty of her was shocking . . . Carl was permitted to make love to *that* body and to kiss *that* face! For God's sake – it seemed wrong. It seemed as if, surely, somebody who was better looking than Carl of the gaunt cheeks and the too lean, even emaciated body, should have had possession of the woman who now lay so still in a drugged unconsciousness.

The sharp awareness of Silver's good looks brought a memory –

In her restless seeking for a man, when she was in college, Marie had never required beauty of male appearance. She had not too high an opinion of her own looks; so she had made an unconscious adjustment in the direction of wanting intelligence in the man. Nothing absolutely displastic, of course, on the physical side. Overweight automatically rejected in a young male person; later – the thought was there – all right. But now, no. And nothing shorter than her own five-five and a half.

Searching. Looking with haunted eyes at the passing faces. Walking. Joining groups. Taking special courses. Casually brushing aside unacceptable masculine hands that reached for her. No sense of being cruel about that.

Suddenly, in her senior year, there was Carl. He was a post graduate student, already possessed of his M.A., heading for a Ph.D. He came out of the murk around her, and reached. And – just like that – she reached back.

In-her there was no thought, ever, of asking where he had been until now. Not the faintest question as to what he might have been doing. In the deeps at the back of her mind was an image of her father, quiet, shrewd, loyal, responsible, slightly satiric, delightful; and Carl looked a little bit like that.

End of search. Oh, she held him off a little bit. And

106

she was always a little startled when she looked into those dark, knowing eyes. But she had infinite trust. Naturally, also, she knew that once you found your guy you slept with him. So, on the third night, she was in bed with an eager, sophisticated male who was visibly startled when his demanding penetration drew a gush of virginal blood.

Unknown to Marie, he went through his usual pattern with this, his 193rd conquest: sex twelve to twenty-five times; no more. Meanwhile, previous girls being phased out, new girls experiencing their first rush.

So unsuspecting Marie was phased out.

It did not *for one minute* cross her mind that she had been captured by a male operator. Used and abused. And dropped. She phoned him as before. He did his normal excusing about studying, and she absolutely accepted his statements as truth itself.

(After a couple of excuses like that, the average young female suddenly gets the message. Feels the awful shock of realization. Has that intense sense of degration and grief. And of course withdraws, and never phones again.)

Marie lived unto herself. In finding Carl, she had confided in no one. In letting him come to her apartment, she had been just a little bit shy and embarrassed about a man staying at her place overnight, so she herself had suggested that he come up the back stairs.

What does a male operator do when he has a trusting innocent on his hands? Carl had had wide-eyed types before, and when they didn't get the thought, he finally, bluntly, told them not to bother him anymore. Naturally, he blamed them. That was always his tactic: get the girl feeling as if there was something wrong with *her*.

What he accused them of was that they had not come to him, pure.

They had been deflowered – he said – before they pretended to fall in love with him ... For God's sake, some of the young women had replied, this is the modern age. What are you? – a male chauvinist ... But they felt guilty. And regretted having had previous experience.

And accepted his rejection.

On a campus where there are thirty thousand students, a male operator can be so hidden that the chances of his accidentally meeting a former girl friend are almost zero. Particularly if he stays away from girls who attend the same classes as he does.

When Marie continued to call, Carl could not accuse *her* of having had other men. Besides – the fact that she had been a virgin until he met her kept niggling at the back of his mind. He had, of course, had a lot of virgins in high school – but not at Marie's age. At twenty-two, as pretty as she was, she was an almost unbelievable find. He phased her out before that really struck him.

But even that realization might merely have led to another period of casual dalliance while he savoured what was by far the simplest super-intelligent pretty girl he had ever met. Instead, an unusual coincidence occurred. On the day that *he* was motivated to call *her*, an automatic female reaction was triggered in Marie. It was not that she was actually suspicious. But she had had *a* thought.

– Really (she told herself, remembering something that somebody had once said, and which she had dismissed at the time as being beneath her ... because, when two people genuinely loved, they didn't have to play games) – really, I was too easy. When a man puts study ahead of sex with a girl, something is lacking in her. Therefore I'm going to have to play hard to get when he finally thinks he has time for me.

A similar type of logic used in physics would never have got her an A in that, her major. But it would not be until years later that an observation in Ms. Craig's unpublished work, *Men Are Doomed*, would finally explain the devastation it wrought upon Carl Hazzard, soon to be a Ph.D. in physics.

He had suddenly got a yearning. Memories came that even he in a way recognized as being slightly exaggerated, of how great it had been to make love to Marie.

So he called her.

She was cool.

He insisted.

She became difficult.

Then her father fell ill; was not expected to live ... come at once. She tried to phone Carl. He was out, of course, making love to another girl. She called far into the wee hours; but Carl didn't come back to his apartment that night.

In the morning she flew off to her father's bedside. And stayed there until he got well. Two and a half weeks later she came back.

While at home she had been doing a lot of what people call thinking, about Carl not being at his apartment at all for an entire sleep period.

– Okay, she thought, so he was out with someone else. *Finis*, by God.

She actually thought of herself as a woman who had come to understand life in a deep sense.

She wouldn't talk to him. She hung up on him. He haunted her doorstep. She called the police and had him removed.

Then she began to hear reports that he was drinking heavily. In fact, he phoned her a couple of times; and his voice had that thick liquory sound.

Fortunately, he had his Ph.D. before this disaster set in.

Then he disappeared.

Marie briskly took her M.A. And then her Ph.D. And who should be at the convocation but a dapper, well-dressed, gaunt, black-eyed, charming young man arrayed in the uniform of a lieutenant commander in the navy, none other than Dr. Carl Hazzard.

'Will you marry me?' he asked.

'When?'

'Now. Tonight. In Reno.'

'Okay.'

The month of honeymoon in Reno had the look of one of those dramatic love affairs that a girl dreams of. A perfect marriage. And then –

He lost interest. (Carl had his own explanation for that.)

Years later, Marie finally read the aphorism by that astute male watcher, Ms. Craig, which referred to such an inversion. It stated simply, 'The terrifying neurosis of the Real Man is that he wants what he can't have, and doesn't want what he can –' (Observation Number 28, *Men Are Doomed*, by Ms. Craig).

Gazing at the limp form of Silver, standing there in her garage – lighted only by a sliver of brightness from the slightly ajar kitchen door, Marie thought: – Silver was hard to get. She was available only if he did some insane thing like going to dead bodies that she knew about.

The analysis seemed true; and it was a lifting thing inside her to have come to such a quick understanding of the situation. Eagerly, Marie went back into her bedroom and secured Silver's purse, where it lay on the floor, and then her own from the drawer of a dresser that was from top to bottom made of gleaming pieces of fine china.

She emptied both purses into two separate little piles on her bed. Within seconds after that she had Silver's address book. And moments later a street name in the peninsula: 4784 Jolson Road ... It's got to be, thought Marie.

Swiftly, she removed from the contents of her own purse anything that might identify who she was. Then she put the stuff back into the two purses.

A minute after that she was in the car. She started the motor, and turned on the headlights. Noticed that she had left the kitchen door ajar. Out of the car for additional seconds to shut and lock it. Back, next, into the driver's seat. Activate with a pushbutton the power that automatically opened the garage door behind the car. Ease the machine backward into the street. Remote-control close and lock the garage door.

And head.

And the shadow ship started to emerge from its shadow. And there was ever so tiny time distortion. And reality twisted ... slightly.

Chapter Thirteen

AFTER THE TIME SHIFT

Basic reality.

Earth shivered in a momentary absence of vibration. For a split moment the solar system wasn't. And then was again.

The split moment was less than a billionth of a second. But a time shift occurred for connected persons. For Marie, who was one of those persons, the process was complex.

. . . Marie struggled up through the pictures and sounds of a dream. Partly awake, finally, but still groggy, she switched on the light and sat up. Her bedside clock showed twenty minutes to one. There was a blue book lying on the bed. Vague surprise, then, as she realized it was not Carl's *Women Are Doomed*.

With a careless flick of the hand, she knocked the volume onto the floor; noticed as it flew through the air that it was a bestseller of several months earlier, *Pimmler's Dummy*, by the celebrated author, Sam Locke . . . How did that get there? I thought I gave it to Mrs. Gray –

She became aware that she was casually stripping off her clothes, tossing them . . . Funny, I must have lain down fully dressed –

Forgot that, also.

She danced lightly over, and stopped, swaying, in front of the ornamented – with gold leaf – full-length mirror that was built in to one of her wall panels. And gazed, entranced, at her unclothed body.

What dimly startled Marie was that she had never done such a thing before in her entire life.

Never looked at herself, nude.

Oh, glances, yes. Unavoidable glimpses while bathing, disrobing, changing into and out of pyjamas. This was

111

different. This time she gazed wide-eyed and with searching intent.

A kind of neural music started to play inside her. And *that* was new, also. She opened her mouth and spoke to the glowing image in the mirror. 'How strange,' she murmured. 'I've never looked at you – ever –

She stopped. What she had unquestionably heard was her own voice. Yet it wasn't. There was a musical lilt in it. Never had that in her whole life.

Standing there, Marie had a vague feeling that she had in the course of the evening made a decision to be like Silver. She couldn't recall the exact moment of deciding that. But the feeling was there.

Was it possible that a mere decision could change something as basic as a voice?

Whatever the cause, no doubt of the effect. An end had been made of drab Marie.

No – consciously, she corrected that, also – the drabness had always been inside her, not outside. Else, those men – like MacKerrie (and earlier, Carl) – wouldn't have kept grabbing her and forcing her over to the bed. To *them*, she must look alive.

Thoughts of MacKerrie and Carl reminded her of Nicer. Happy again, she loped over to the phone, and dialled his number. For some reason, she was not surprised when his voice came on, and said one of those non-identifying things. But it was his voice.

Marie, who by now was deliciously ensconced under the satin sheets, and still deliciously without clothes, said in that trilling musical voice, 'Marie speaking, Phil. Hope it isn't too late for a call.'

Not that simple. For Nicer, the time was several weeks before he had met Marie – except for long ago when his father was still on the board of the Non-Pareil Corporation. But he recognized a shadow condition and an hormonic voice when it manifested, and deduced the rest. So he said, 'Who is this?'

'Marie – of course.' The lilting voice suddenly uncertain.

Nicer braced himself. The next question was going to be

112

decisive. 'I know several Maries but none has a voice like yours.'

– True, Marie thought cosily. No one has ever heard my Silver-ized voice before.

'Marie Hazzard.'

Nicer did not make the mistake of saying, 'Oh – Hazzard Laboratories!' But all kinds of future possibilities were falling in place. What he said was, 'Where shall we meet?'

Marie falsely remembered that Silver was sleeping in the next room. (That wouldn't be for several weeks.) 'The hotel,' she said.

'Got the name straight?' he asked.

'Of course. The Westermore.'

'And the room number?'

'815.' Joyously.

'Okay. See you.'

Nicer disconnected. And hastily called Hotel Westermore, and asked for a reservation for room 815.

It was occupied.

Hastily, he called Somebody Important, who called the hotel owner. A deal was made whereby the occupants of room 815 accepted $500 in cash, the hotel's apologies, and another room free, and moved. All in ten minutes.

Marie slipped into panties, glided into a nothing dress, stepped into high heels, and wrapped a coat around her . . . Really, she thought, a woman can be decent in one minute –

It took another minute to check her purse. Seconds after that she was tiptoeing past Carl's apartment, where she had left Silver sleeping. In the garage, a momentary puzzlement. Her Mercedes was not there. The dismissing thought came rapidly: John must have come late, and taken it, and was having something done to it in one of those all-night garages.

John was a technician-employee who was paid extra to keep an eye on the cars, and make sure they were always in top condition and appearance.

For Marie, it was no problem to climb grandly into Carl's seldom-used Cadillac . . .

Arrived at the hotel, she went straight upstairs like any

113

proper guest. The key Nicer had given her worked. So her coming was all very discreet, as it should be; no one noticing the singing body, and no one speaking in a way that she had to answer.

She undressed and lay in the bed without any clothes on, and presently had a faraway thought from deep in her mind where the old Marie was sleeping but not dead. From that depth came the first argument against the automaticness and shamelessness of what she was doing, in the form of an aphoristic pun.

She smiled, and spoke it in all its greatness into the silence of the room: 'You cannot keep a good woman down – for long. So you'd better hurry, Philip Nicer.'

Within instants after she finished speaking, as if her words were the signal, a key moved softly in the door. When it opened, moments later, the man was briefly silhouetted against the hall light. And it was he.

Then he was inside, and the door closed behind him. Marie was aware of him coming towards her. The room suffered from a few glints of light coming through the drawn blinds; so she could see him as he walked towards her. Even in that almost night, there was a way he held himself – a Real Man, she thought.

It reminded her slightly of Carl. An impression of strength and determination. He sank down on the edge of the bed beside her. That close she could see he was smiling.

Still smiling, he bent down toward her. She braced ever so slightly. But it was a very soft-lipped kiss that he gave her.

When the kiss ended, he drew away, and up, and back into the darkness. She heard his undressing movements.

His body, she discovered, was much firmer than MacKerrie's, as she clearly recalled it, or Carl's – as she vaguely remembered it. Much firmer. Much.

He was not heavy. But the all-over hardness of him was an unexpected and surprisingly pleasant shock. She felt an enormous vitality from him.

Yet for a while he talked more than he acted.

Questions.

Her mind, each question, went off somewhere. When,

114

between kisses, he asked more questions, what he asked was not what she talked about.

She didn't remember what he said. And, presently, he seemed amused by that. After that it was man-woman.

... Marie watched as Nicer, fully dressed, emerged from the bathroom. He came over to her, and he did something wonderfully significant. He bent down and drew the sheet up over her nude body, which she had left exposed.

Marie was delighted ... He's embarrassed by the way I responded –

The man continued to gaze down at her, which was an effectively handsome thing for him to do. Impressed, Marie trilled at him in her now shamelessly musical voice, 'A penny for your thoughts, Colonel?'

He smiled, sort of sadly. 'I guess we'll just have to play this, blind,' he said. 'You're like a bird on the wing. This is not the moment to ask you what it would be like if your wings were clipped. Or –' he rephrased it – 'what it *was* like?'

'The way *I* feel is, you'd better get back into this bed.'

He thought, awed: – The hormones are really dancing ...

Aloud, he said, 'Marie, listen. You should know some facts. This condition will continue for six days. During that time I will be around. So, no matter where you find yourself, no matter how strange, remember I'll be nearby somewhere. Got that?' He smiled to take the implied threat out of what he was saying. Threat not by him, but *to* her.

Again, if she heard, if the words went in and made any contact at all – it didn't show. But she gave him an answering smile. And she said, 'You're cute.'

Oddly, her voice, though it was still musical, rang in her ears with a peculiar hollow echoing. And she felt – felt – felt –

... The shadow ...

Chapter Fourteen

VICTIM OF THE GAS GUN

... Jolson Road was in the hills at the south end of the city. Marie turned into a driveway between two high posterns, and followed a paved road for several hundred yards. It came abruptly into a courtyard of the kind of house that Marie had seen at the ancestral homes of the Old South, and – on her two visits to England – the mansions of the old nobility.

Long, wide, three stories high, built of brick and stone, perfectly kept, enframed in a garden – the residence of a very rich man.

She arrived at the front entrance, and stopped. There were – she could see – lights on in the house, and there were lights on the front porch. But she did not actually sight a living person. No shadowy figures pulled aside drapes to peer out of windows. Nobody came to the door.

It suggested that the sound of an arriving car did not arouse the suspicion of whoever was inside.

Marie got out of the car, walked to the door, and rang. Then rang again. Then again, more insistently.

The door did not open. Somebody spoke at her through a speaker system. 'Who is it?'

'Silver is hurt,' said Marie.

The man who had inquired did not trouble to turn off the speaker, as he called off at somebody else: 'It's a woman. She's got Silver with her. She says Silver is hurt.'

The other voice must have come nearer, for it was suddenly audible. 'Hurt?' it said. It sounded shocked.

'Better be careful,' cautioned the first voice. 'Remember what's going on here tonight.'

The door opened a crack, and came to a stop against a chain. A face peered out. It was the face of a man of about fifty.

'Who are you?' he asked in a firm, determined voice.

'I'm a friend of Silver's,' said Marie. 'Before she fainted, she told me to bring her here.'

'Where is she?'

'She's on the floor in the back seat of the car.'

The door shut. There was silence. Marie deduced that the speaker system had been shut off, and that the two men were consulting. What they were doing seemed incredibly normal. Night. A strange visitor. An outlying residence. They were being careful. Could these people really be alienoid invaders?

There was another wispy thought: – What am I doing here? Am I out of my mind? . . . The blankness closed down on those questions, blotting them.

The door opened, revealing a wide, bright hallway, and seven well-dressed men. Four of the men came out. As Marie stepped aside, the four went by her down to her car. They opened the rear door, and looked in. At which point one of them turned and called, 'It's Silver all right.'

At that the fiftyish man came out onto the porch. He ignored Marie. A feminine something inside her resented that. Impelled by that feeling, she half-turned, and moved a little, so that if he glanced in her direction he would see her profile – which, from comments made by men, she had decided was her best physical asset.

Realization of what she was doing came moments after that. Instant shame . . . Did it again – She recognized it as an attempt to solicit a man's protective interest, incited by her attractive appearance.

Marie stood beside the big man, and watched as three of the men carried Silver up the steps and into the house. They laid her on a gleaming bench in that big hall. One of the men inside went over, picked up her wrist, and checked her pulse against his wrist watch. Then he reached and pulled back an eyelid.

A doctor? Evidently. For he turned, and said, 'Her pulse is too normal for a faint. It could be certain types of drugs. But my guess is a gas gun was used on her. Heart beat is regular, so I'd deduce it was one of the –' He named a group of chemicals. 'The effect doesn't last much over an hour, so she should be coming to shortly.'

Marie had been listening intently to the swift, accurate analysis. Momentarily, she forgot the older man who had come out onto the porch. She remembered him with a start as strong fingers caught her wrist, and tugged at her. The firm voice said into her left ear, 'You'd better come inside, Ms.'

He didn't wait for her to walk in by herself. She felt herself drawn forward into the house. As she stepped across the threshold, one of the three men who had helped carry Silver into the house said, 'Do you think she knows what happened to Silver?'

There was no problem about that. Marie had during the past few moments been thinking hard about that very thing. She said now, simply, 'The doorbell rang. When I answered it, this strange woman staggered in, and fell. Before she passed out, she told me not to take her to the doctor's, but to bring her down here.' She paused, and then spoke the lie she had made up on the way down, 'I'm Betty Fardell.' It was the name of a college classmate.

The M.D. type laughed curtly at her explanation, and said in a ridiculing tone, 'Paul, with a gas capsule she wouldn't have got to that door, or had a chance to give an address. Besides –' coldly – 'it's time you face up to what Silver is –'

The big man cut off the words with an impatient gesture. He said, 'Let's get her up to her bedroom.' To Marie, he said courteously, 'Thank you, Miss Fardell. Will you come up with us and temporarily baby-sit Silver? We're very busy here tonight, but I'll come in soon.'

... And there, bare minutes later, Marie was in a bedroom, with the door closed.

Alone with Silver.

It was really an unacceptable situation; so it seemed to Marie. For over fourteen years, she had avoided to the best of her knowledge ever being in the same room with a Carl Hazzard mistress. In fact she had once made an aphorism of her own on that very subject:

'One way you can tell a Real Man is by the fact that he believes it is mature for his First Wife and his Second Wife to accept being brought into each other's homes. And he

118

would just love to have a roomful of his mistresses all babbling away to each other; and he sitting there smugly with The Knowledge: I-got-'em-all-by-God-and-that-proves-something.'

Marie had her own idea of what it proved. But that was not part of the written-down aphorism. In fact, her view on that godly state of the conquering male was one of her few unprintable judgments.

For a while, feeling essentially blank, she sat in an armchair beside the fancy bed. But she finally had a thought: – I'd better search this room before Silver comes to . . .

With that, she was up at once. The search was disappointing. Another wealthy woman's room, much like her own – that was the outcome. Spacious. High-ceilinged. Furnished with expensive modern furniture, exquisitely beautiful like its owner.

Before returning to her armchair, Marie went to the door and tried to open it. It was locked.

Sitting down again, her situation unimproved, except now she *knew* she was a prisoner.

– I still, she told herself, have my gas capsule discharger . . . And she had noticed a pistol in one of the drawers of a bureau – I suppose I ought to get that before Silver awakens and plops me with it.

But – with a sigh – she didn't really believe that would happen. So she didn't move.

Chapter Fifteen

THE ROBOT REMEMBERS

Gannott entered the room where Carl was sitting, so to
say, on his motionless wheels. The Deean leader nodded at
the guard. 'Take a break, if you wish, Don.' The other
man evidently found this an attractive idea, for he got up
and made his exit.

The big man had no fear of his captive. Engineers had
gingerly removed the cannon-rifle on top of Carl, and of
course no one had reconnected him to the vehicle control.
For nearly twenty-four hours, earth's only bodiless brain
had been literally as helpless as it was possible for
anything, or anybody, to be.

As Gannott approached, he grabbed a chair in his
pathway, and presently placed it in front of the brain
machine. But he remained standing.

These preliminaries, brief though they were, gave Carl
time to disconnect from the viewing camera in the Hazzard
house. And to orient again to his prison.

'Hello, Dr. Carl,' Gannott said.

'Hello,' replied the machine voice.

The two beings – Paul Gannott, the Deean alienoid
who looked human, and Carl Hazzard, the human being
whose brain was encased in a machine, stared at each
other, one with eyes and the other by way of a TV-type
camera.

Apparently satisfied, Gannott sat down, and said, 'If you
don't mind I'd like to light a cigarette and talk to you.'

Carl, who of course had all the time in the world, and
was only, perversely, worried over what Marie was doing
with *her* time, expressed his willingness. But he was wary.
From the beginning, Gannott had shown as an unusually
impressive person and as a remorseless leader.

Something new here; that was his observation. Another

purpose, different from what had developed from their conversation after he was first captured.

He found himself remembering his lifetime adult view: that even when men were discussing business they were really reflecting their woman situation. The tone of voice, the freedom – or lack of it – with which they could momentarily consider such a drab matter as the sale of goods or a scientific research programme, the tensions in the body, gestures, movements, twistings – everything was always an exact image of a man's only true obsession: sex . . . Carl believed.

Gannott said, 'Something about your role in this matter puzzles me.'

'Which something?'

The heavy face was intent. 'Have you any explanation for why our ship would want to take you along to Deea?'

Unexpected question. Brief blankness. Then the first thought stirring that was not a part of the fantasy state into which he had been precipitated at the prospect of isolating Marie away from all other men forever.

Finally: 'I haven't the faintest –' Carl began, and then as a startled thought came, he finished weakly – 'idea.'

The stunning thought was: – I was briefly in direct communication with the ship's robotic centre when I plugged into it. *It remembers me . . .*

It seemed to him that something about that contact was motivating the machine out there in some automatic way related to its programming.

Gannott was fumbling in his pocket. His hand emerged with what looked like a photograph. 'I have the picture of a woman here,' he said. 'I wonder if you'd look at her and tell me if you recognize her.'

He stood up and walked forward until he stood directly in front of the electronic 'eye' through which Carl viewed the world from that side.

The first photo that Gannott held out was of Marie. It had been taken by an automatic camera as she walked through the front door of the Gannott mansion half an hour before. Carl recognized her at once, naturally. And since he hoped that Marie would join him in about twenty-four hours, he promptly identified her.

The second photo was of Silver lying unconscious on the hall bench. Her face was half-turned toward the camera, and so was sufficiently visible for identification. Carl recognized her at once as the woman he had seen for the first time in his apartment about an hour before. Since his previous relationship had been so intimate, though always in the darkness of a bedroom at night, he naturally had no intention of admitting any knowledge whatsoever. Thus, after a suitable pause, he made his total denial.

With that, it was Gannott's turn to react. His impulse was to say, 'If that is true, Dr. Carl, then how would you explain the fact that your wife brought her here a little while ago?'

He didn't say it. The exact moment of such a confrontation, it seemed to Gannott, should be carefully prepared for, so that all relevant information would automatically be evoked. After what seemed only moments, he replaced the photographs in his breast pocket. He stood, then, struggling to suppress a smile of triumph.

Finally: 'If you will wait here,' he said, 'I'll bring in someone else.'

He walked to the corridor door, opened it, and went out, leaving the door ajar. A minute went by. Then he came back, followed after moments only by three men. Of these latter, two were guards of the third, who had his hands tied behind his back.

The third man was about as grim an individual as any man could ever be. But he took one look at the six-wheeled machine that stood in the corner across from the door. And he cried out involuntarily, 'Carl!'

'Mac!' said the machine, sounding equally startled.

The prisoner was Angus MacKerrie, M.D.

MacKerrie's voice was darkly angry. 'I was kidnapped as I was leaving the Brain Foundation, and brought over here.'

'But why? – what? –'

'I haven't the faintest idea. The whole thing is utterly mad.'

Paul Gannott watched the confrontation, and could not restrain a smile of triumph. He walked forward, and said:

'I'm sure you will agree, Doctor, that for such a long journey, a disembodied brain should have expert care. Who better than Dr. Angus MacKerrie, the man who performed the operation and knows what must be done. We shall be happy to furnish any equipment which the two of you in consultation agree that you will need. Food and other supplies suitable for human beings are already aboard. I understand from our earlier conversation that you were accidentally rendered immobile. Dr. MacKerrie has my authority to reconnect you to this six-wheeled vehicle. Thus you will be mobile again and be able to traverse the numerous corridors of the large vessel which will transport you to Deea.'

He was smiling by the time he had finished. He said, 'As you can see, we Deeans aren't all bad, despite our reputations.'

He stepped back. As he turned away, he said, 'If you'll excuse me again.'

He left the room hastily.

Gannott went upstairs. With a twisted smile, he presently unlocked the door of Silver's bedroom. 'Miss Fardell,' he began in a silken tone, as he entered, 'I would like you to come –'

At this point his voice faltered. The smile vanished. Gulping, he charged all the way inside. Plunged wildly to the right wall, then to the left. Peered under the bed, behind settees, into clothes closets.

But in the end there was no doubt. The two women had disappeared. The stunned Deean leader hastened back to Carl and MacKerrie. 'It has become necessary,' he said, 'to have you both taken up to the ship right away.' He gestured at his aides. 'Take them away!' he commanded.

Carl was wheeled out into the night by half a dozen men through a brightly lighted patio, across a courtyard, and into a dark area. MacKerrie and his guards followed.

What they came to was not easy to see, since it was in an unlighted space. A shape somewhat like a beehive, the top of which was more pointed than a hive. This structure was roughly twenty feet in diameter and fifteen feet high. There in the darkness it sat on the soil of earth.

A ramp slanted from the ground to a shadowy entrance five feet up. Up this ramp walked MacKerrie and up it the men pushed Carl.

Some of the men came down the ramp again. Those that stayed aboard – four in all – firmly lashed Carl to some sturdy stanchions. Then, along with MacKerrie, they sat down in cushioned seats that looked quite ordinary, and fastened seat belts.

A faint wheezing sound was the next ordinary thing. Now, the object did a totally extraordinary, colossal process. It lifted into the night sky. It had no wings, no rockets. But up it went.

The night sky was clouded, but there was some visibility. Presumably, a passerby, or a nearby resident could have glanced up and noticed the shadowy, silent module as it raised itself. But if anyone did see, it was not apparent in the first decisive minute. After that it was of course too late.

Chapter Sixteen

AN 8-P ACCOMPLISHED

Unnoticing Carl.

He virtually ignored the entire lift process.

Suddenly, the reality underlying his fantasy surfaced from that nether depth where, of course, it had been pulsating and palpitating all these hours since the initial excitement about it had hit him the previous night.

Alone with Marie for every conscious moment of fifty years. That was the promise from Gannott that had just about loosed his brain from its mechanical container. The excitement that came at that moment had no relation to reality at all.

Even now that he was 'better', he didn't notice that. It did not occur that the Marie whose presence he craved was the woman to whom he had once, contemptuously, offered all his Wednesday evenings – after 10 p.m. And that maybe she remembered that and wouldn't appreciate his company. In those days, when he was to all outward appearances a whole man, he had been driven by erotic impulses so feverish that he had never for a minute asked himself why, or how, or what.

And he didn't really ask now. Images sort of winked through his mind. The detectives he had hired to watch her during his . . . great . . . years, when sometimes she and he didn't eat a meal at the same table for weeks. His insane suspicion, unwarranted distrust, outrageous accusations and false fury, which went on for *years* – the memories of that flickered past his mind's eye, but made only a weak impression. Didn't seem all that bad. An unfortunate game, he called it now.

The awfulest irony of that game, of course, he didn't know. For almost a decade and a half he had sardonically accepted that she was really living a blank virginal existence; and his thought had been that, if he persisted with his game, one of these years she would break down, and, rather than have nothing, agree to the limited relationship that he was prepared to offer. She must realize – that had been his thought – that something was better than a lifetime of nothing.

And so he had made his wild threat that he would name Dr. Walter Drexel as his murderer – and as her lover (which would implicate her).

At last, that finally broke the barriers inside Marie. To save herself, she became, unknown to Carl, the mistress of Dr. Angus MacKerrie.

Although he had made occasional revolting remarks about MacKerrie to Marie, truth was that of the various men of his and Marie's acquaintance, Carl had never devoted any real suspicion to MacKerrie. What the surgeon did with his personal life had not seriously crossed Carl's mind. Presumably, MacKerrie had a woman – or women – out there in the great city. But Carl had never been curious.

All in an instant that vagueness was penetrated. The prospect of MacKerrie coming along on the fifty-year journey brought an horrendous mental image of Marie and MacKerrie as the only human, body-possessing couple ... For God's sake, they'll have no alternative but to seek each other's companionship –

The qualm was utterly convincing to an ex-sex maniac like Carl. After his initial enthusiasm for the trip, he had already had second thoughts. And third. And fourth. Yet, since there seemed no escape from these determined alienoids, he merely made his attempt to contact Marie more directly: by peering hopefully through the TV camera eye in his part of their house. And she had actually come into the room, but in her typical maddening fashion – never giving him a thought – had not noticed. But there was a second plan, another hope, earlier mentally put off until midnight.

No putting off now. The Deeans, in capturing him, had also transported the specially built van in which he had made his two dangerous journeys. Swiftly, Carl interconnected with the van mechanism. And saw presently that the vehicle was parked inside a high fence besides a building (the Gannott house?) There were many other cars nosed in parallel to his.

Carl made a swift, four-sided survey of the parking lot. Saw no movement. And acted without delay. He started the motor, waited half a minute for it to warm up, then eased it backward out of the parking space. He had intended, if necessary, to break forcibly *through* the wooden fence and charge out onto the nearby street. But, as he completed his backing manoeuvre, he saw that there was a driveway leading through trees. Silently, his van rolled along it, and emerged onto a residential street. Carl turned it north. At the first corner, he paused, and backed up until he could read the street signs: Jolson Road and 18th Avenue.

With that, he was off, his destination the valley home of Police Lieutenant Barry Turcott – the only man that he could think of that he could trust. What he could do with Turcott, or Turcott could do for him when he got him across the considerable distance from one end of a large city to the other, was not clear.

But he had no other meaningful hope.

He was still considering what he might do, still on a darkened street heading toward a still distant freeway on-ramp, when another car, a black sedan, emerged from a side avenue, and swerved in behind him.

The very next instant, a thin beam of light reached out from the hood of the bigger car and bridged the distance to Carl's van. Bright, oh, bright, but pencil thin, the beam. Carl could not see where it touched his vehicle. But the van tilted and began the developing wobble that sickeningly signalled a flar, rear tyre.

Mere moments later, the swaying and tendency to out-of-controllness convinced that normally cynical but persistent philosopher, Dr. Carl Hazzard, that the game was up.

Appalled but resigned, he slowed even more, edged bumpily toward the curb, and stopped. Since he was curious, he maintained his connection with the disabled van while the sedan drew up alongside. The two men in the front seat of the car did not get out. Nor did they lower their windows.

Pause. Then a spindle-shaped glinting device reared into view. It also came out of some recess in the hood, but this time from near the windshield. The brightness that flashed from it seemed to leap from the spindle into the driver of Carl's van. Carl, deducing murder intent, allowed the dummy to sink back against the seat.

Hastily, he now turned up the volume on the directional microphone system at that side of the van. What he picked up by this means was blurred. But he heard it. Inside the closed car, the man beside the driver said, 'Brother Metnov.'

The reply came from a speaker system somewhere in the front seat. 'Metnov speaking, brother.'

The voice that uttered these stereotypes was a muffled baritone. But it had a quality in it ... different. Hearing that quality, Carl had the thought: who could be *that* confident?

The first voice was speaking again: 'An 8-P accomplished, brother.'

'Good.'

'Only one so far.'

'Can't do better than a hundred per cent,' said the 'great' voice of 'Brother' Metnov.

'Where are you now, brother?'

'Code 8-A.'

'Any developments?'

'Not since 8-G.' The voice added firmly, 'Goodbye, brother.'

'Goodbye, Brother Metnov.'

There was the silence, evidently, of disconnection. Then the voice of the driver said matter-of-factly, 'Better call Susan, Horace, and tell her you'll be home late.'

'What about you calling Muriel?'

'Are you out of your mind? If she gets me on a line she'll want me to prove where I am. I –'

The fadeout was swift because the machine had started forward. Its taillights receded rapidly into the dark distance of the tree-lined street.

Carl stayed connected – for a while. Until vague awareness began to come, then, of what was happening where his 'body' was. He finally let the impressions come through. And made his switch of attention from the useless van back to . . . himself.

Barely in time to see the finale of the journey on a screen inside the lift. There, in the near distance, a long, dark shape was visible. The big vessel seemed in the manner of space objects to drift closer.

At first, Carl merely watched dully, thinking all the time of Marie and MacKerrie. Then as, only seconds later, the thing out there took on the size of a small mountain, his scientific interest was finally, if briefly, stirred.

The fascination, and absorption, came as the colossus became a curving metal wall at least a thousand feet high and some indeterminate but immensely greater length: half a mile, even two thirds, he guessed roughly.

Before he could make a more precise estimate, the module drifted too close for an overall view. Because of the blank wall effect, then, it was not obvious at what point the outer wall merely loomed above and below and to every side, and when the module actually entered an equally dark and hard-to-make-out airlock.

Chapter Seventeen

WHITE HELLFIRE IN THE COMPUTER

Marie followed Silver because there was nothing else to do.

The younger woman had opened her eyes several minutes before. Looked around with darting gaze. Eyes widened as she evidently recognized where she was. She had sat up with a convulsive movement of her long, lean body.

Swiftly, in a low voice, and without showing any antagonism over what had happened, she described the coming of the ship, *Takeover*. And what that coming meant.

Then she slid off the bed, and whispered to Marie, 'I assume that now you've absolutely got to help me do what has to be done.'

Marie was not yet at the speaking level with Silver. She merely mutely nodded.

. . . Amazing that none of her earlier feeling against this woman remained. The absolutely automatic reaction of firing the gas capsule discharger at Silver seemed exactly that to her now: Automatic. And of course irrational.

The thought ended. Silver was running, heading toward the farthest away clothes closet. She literally jerked the door open. As swiftly turned a light on. And then fumbled forward past a slew of fluffy feminine clothes items, and did something else.

Marie, who had followed her, involuntarily said, 'Oooo.'

A part of the rear of the closet had silently folded out of sight. Visible beyond was a dimly lighted passageway.

Silver beckoned Marie, and as Marie entered and also gingerly pressed past the wall-to-wall clothing, Silver whispered, 'I had this built one time when Paul went away. Used the same contractor as the one Carl used for that entrance to his –'

She stopped. In the brilliant light that poured down from the clothes closet ceiling, her blue eyes widened at her indiscretion. Then she shrugged. 'I guess I'm not fully alert yet. Where is Carl, anyway? We really need a man to do what has to be done here.'

Marie parted her lips to explain Carl's condition. And closed them again, shocked. The thought: – She doesn't know about him . . .

Confused thoughts about what a woman might feel, who had been a mistress to what was now a mechanized brain. Momentary impulse to hit Silver with the information as a punishment. But that feeling also faded quickly.

She managed finally to gulp, 'We're on our own.' A thought about the situation came into her mind. She hesitated, and then spoke it: 'Two women,' she said, 'without a single knight errant. And of course,' she added firmly, 'for what we do tonight, we shall not have to pay the price in the time-honoured way of a woman.'

'I'll have a comment on that in a moment,' said the other woman. 'Right now –' She leaned back – 'will you go past me? I want to lock things up behind us.'

Moments after Marie had done so, there was Silver; and the secret entrance was folded back into position. The younger woman whispered, 'The closet side is covered with my sloppiest dresses. Men seldom poke around in swishy stuff like that unless there's a woman inside it. Now – here.'

She reached up to a shelf and lifted down a stick-like metallic object which she pushed into Marie's reluctant hands. 'That's a Sleele plint,' she said. 'To get it I paid that time-honoured price you just mentioned to the Sleele leader here on earth, a man named Metnov.'

Marie noticed both implications of the remark: *The Sleele leader on earth* . . . There was nothing to think about that at the moment. So that passed her by, swiftly. But about the other part, the woman part – she had a series of peculiar thoughts. Very rapid. With an odd, startled feeling of being aware, literally for the first time in her life, that there was another attitude that a woman could have toward men. Other, that is, than being automatic.

That second awareness also grew blurry. Yielded to the weight of the thing that had been placed in her hand.

The object was heavier than Marie expected. It *looked* not precisely fluffy but gave the impression of something hollow and thin and therefore light. But it was at least as weighty as her purse. To hold it properly, she had to grasp it firmly – she realized. Which she continued to resist doing. The stick half-lay in her fingers, but was other-half held.

'Point that like a gun,' Silver said *sotto voce*, 'and press the little button near your finger. It goes off with a plop. But it sure is effective for several hundred yards.'

Marie had parted her lips to say rejectingly, 'I still have my gas capsule discharger.' But the words never issued forth. Because the meaning of 'several hundred yards' penetrated. Since the gas discharger was effective for less than fifty feet, at that point her fingers tightened on the . . . plint. 'I've got it,' said Marie.

Silver made no immediate, further comment. Instead, she started along the passageway, and only after a while flung a question over her shoulder: 'Can you incapacitate a computer?'

'Depends,' said Marie, 'on what kind it is. 'But –' Pause – 'what good will that do? It's the ship up there that's dangerous.'

'If we wreck this computer tonight,' said Silver, 'it will delay the attack until the people who are here in this house can get over to another computer on the east coast or to a third in Texas. All these machines interact with other machines. We can gain a day's delay.'

An enormous psychic weight was lifting from Marie. Silver awakening had brought a plan to find Carl, and a hope that she could reconnect him back into control of his mobile unit. That last was an even vaguer hope than the plan. During the entire year of Carl's martyrdom she had never looked inside the mechanism that housed him. Had avoided *knowing* details about his insides. Had left that to MacKerrie and his Brain Foundation technicians.

Suddenly, now, she knew one thing she *could* do. The computer. A tiny restriction about *that*, also. She loved

132

perfect machines; hated to see them not working, or damaged. Surely, that did not apply in this situation. She gulped, 'Let's go!' in an overstimulated 'go' tone.

Swift response. Silver grabbed her arm. 'My God, you're brave,' she whispered. 'I'm terrified that my husband will finally find out what I'm up to.'

Marie was silent. Receptive in a vague way.

Silver babbled on, *sotto voce*, 'The poor guy – my husband – decided to level with me. Decided to treat me, as he called it, like a mature woman. I thought I had married a wealthy banker – which, of course, was and is true, too – but then he told me about his being a human-looking alienoid. About being a Deean. And that there were on earth six or seven groups from different galactic races that know each other. I haven't the faintest notion what Paul really expected of me. I think he had some feeling – it was his analysis of earth women – that he was catering to some basic need in me to be married to a superior male. Out of his mind. I immediately got the feeling that I had to save earth at no matter what cost to me. For God's sake, if I was going to marry an alienoid because he was better than human, why would I choose a Deean? There are at least three, or even four, advanced races here that are superior to the Deeans. So if I had a choice – and I was interested, which I'm not – I'd take a Sleele, or, better still, a Luind. They're the tops, and apparently differ from each other in that Sleeles are rats and the Luinds have basically good intentions. The Luind leader is cute, and proved his integrity. When I offered myself to him, he turned me down. Said he didn't play around with the wives of other Galactics. First time anybody ever rejected me. It piqued me, but it felt honest.'

As the whispered confession concluded, they reached a stairway. Silver led the way down. Marie followed, thinking: – It's not that I'm brave. It's just, I don't want to be made love to by that S.O.B. MacKerrie even one more time . . .

The intense emotion of that reaction startled her. A minute scientific awareness was stirred in her brain . . . Just one moment, she thought, during the entire year that

133

it was happening, I didn't fight that hard, or feel that vindictive –

She had an abrupt, incredible realization: – I'm trying to convince Philip Nicer somewhere inside me that the MacKerrie thing didn't mean anything. No, no, worse, I'm trying to persuade him *it didn't happen.*

She was shocked because – fantastically – the underlying belief was that she belonged to Philip Nicer.

For a reason fleetingly connected with the thought she had had earlier about Silver's attitude ... it took only seconds to argue herself out of that submissively feminine concept.

Down two narrow flights of stairs they went – an amazing secret passageway, clandestinely constructed by a capable builder at Silver's behest. By being a beautiful, available sex object, Silver had modified this enemy stronghold. Penetrated its security. Shattered its defences.

And so the two women presently stood in a long basement room at one end of the gleaming computer that Carl had seen that first night. The make of the machine was not immediately recognizable to Marie's educated eyes. But her roving gaze swiftly located the fuse box.

It was the work of a minute to remove the panel. A single sweeping glance established that the fuses were of varying resistances. Her fingers flashed. Removed high, and inserted low. Switched low to high.

Even as she did so, the machine's alarm system uttered a series of screeches. And lights blinked on. Flashing. Coloured. Somewhere, a man's voice yelled, 'Good God, what's that?'

Across the room, two attendants entered from a door. By that time there was a rumbling sound from the computer, and a hissing. Abruptly, the room was warmer.

A destruct system! ... She had triggered it. Marie, pale, whispered, 'Hurry! We've got to get out of here!'

They had been backing away. Now, they crouched low, and, turning, ran for the secret entrance. As that metal door silently folded shut behind them, Marie had one last glimpse of what they were leaving in the basement. A long line of blue-white fire was showing *through* the metal of the computer. During that fleeting look at the total disaster she had caused, she heard a man's hoarse scream.

The door closed tight, and sealed away the basement. But it could not seal off her memory of what she had seen. Nor could it stop her continuing awareness of what must be happening back there, still.

By that time they were climbing the narrow stairs, and they were both breathing hard. Silver gasped, 'This thing has an exit in one of the guest cabins at the rear of the house. We'll have to make our way from there to a car I've got hidden.'

The picture in Marie's mind had grown absolutely horrifying. The house! Those two men! She had a mental visualization of a white hellfire breaking through the computer's steel walls and burning up the men in a single burst of unendurable heat blast. And then – and then – burning up the house with equal irresistible, ravaging power. Nothing could withstand the intense energy that she had glimpsed in that one backward look.

– Oh, God! she thought, Carl is in there somewhere, helpless. What have I done? . . .

The tears were spurting, almost blinding her, as Silver opened the door in the closet of the guest cabin. They emerged moments later into a neatly furnished bed-sitting room. At once Marie was at the window, gazing avidly toward the house. She pressed her face against the glass.

The scene which her eyes, figuratively, devoured was peaceful. From the cottage window she could see a garden, a swimming pool, and then the long rear of the residence. The entire place was brightly lighted inside and out, all the windows shining forth, and strings of other shiningnesses outside. Not exactly like day; but a reasonable facsimile.

Marie's eyes flicked toward what – she guessed – were the basement windows. Cringed in anticipation. But – nothing. Not a sign of the hideous fire that she had started.

She thought, relieved: – The destruct fuel must have burned itself out . . . And that would simply leave the over-heated metal sitting there on that concrete floor under a shielded ceiling. The whole beginning its long cooling process.

The whispered words of Silver touched her ear. 'I'm awfully glad you're the one that has the plint.'

Marie was astonished. 'Whatever for?' In her amazement, she spoke in her normal voice.

'Be sure,' admonished Silver, 'to have it ready when we go outside.'

The implication that they would be in danger out there brought a chill to Marie. Involuntarily, her grip tightened on the weapon.

Silver spoke again, also in a normal voice, 'I'm a woman who is willing for a man to do whatever fighting has to be done. I don't want to do any of it myself. So if there's trouble, I wouldn't be able to shoot anyway. But you can. Your training as a physicist proves that you're more willing to be involved in a man's world.'

– Nothing, thought Marie, wryly, like being told that you're a masculine woman and not a feminine one ... A fleeting wonder came, about the fantastic risks that Silver had taken all these years. But, true, it was men she had tried to motivate. Men like Carl and – who else had she said? – the Sleele leader on earth. And, since she had also offered herself to the ... Luind ... leader, presumably that same offer had been made to still other men, who, presumably, had not turned her down. And who had – also presumably – gone out to act and do in return for the use of that slinky body afterwards.

Marie was shocked.

But there was a thought-feeling inside her, a numbness over what had already happened ... I should be at home, Marie thought tearfully, and in bed with a man letting him make love to me, if that's what he wants – and, of course, that's what he would want ... And when he's satisfied, he'll have a natural impulse to charge out here into this dangerous area, and do deeds of derring-do –

Somehow, she could not help but feel that men did this kind of madness with more sense than women. They hid better. They knew when to dive for the floor. And they could crawl along on their stomachs while under fire.

Whereas Silver and she hadn't dived even once. Nor did it seem to have occurred to them that crawling was safer.

These numerous skit*ering thoughts ended, as Silver whispered, 'I've got to take into account that we could be stopped when we go outside. So I'd better make a certain phone call right now. You get on that bedroom extension, will you, and listen in.'

'Who are you going to call?'

'You'll see.'

Chapter Eighteen

DEATH FROM THE PLINT

Silver sank down in the chair beside the phone, dialled operator, and asked for Paris.

A strange feeling was in Marie's head as she settled on the bed, and picked up the phone. She was glad for the chance to slump, with the extension instrument in her lap.

The connection went through with surprising speed. Marie's educated ear heard altogether three relays close in rapid order. Then a man's vibrant voice came on. 'Metnov,' it said; and Marie actually jumped. There was a male quality in that voice that seemed to go right through her body.

'Silver here.'

If the person behind that electrifying male voice was taken aback, it didn't show. 'What's on your mind, Beautiful Silver?'

'Anton,' said Silver, 'this Deean takeover plan is driving me out of my mind. And I want you to do something about it.'

'Such as what?' Utterly relaxed tone.

'I want you to stop it.'

'Now, darling, it would take me a year to get a ship here that could handle the monster machine that's up there.'

'I don't believe it. Now, listen –' Firmly – 'I want a promise from you right now. Or else.'

'Else what?'

'I'll tell Paul everything.'

'Well, we couldn't have that,' smiled the voice. 'So, all right, I promise.'

'I don't believe you.' Suddenly, the singing voice sounded uncertain.

'You wanted my promise. I've made it.'

'Well –' defensively – 'you don't sound sincere.'

138

'Sleeles never do –' same smiling tone – 'You've said so, yourself.'

'True.' Silver seemed to be bracing against her sudden qualms. 'Well, you'd better mean it. Because I *am* just about out of my mind. And so I'm capable of what I said –'

'You've convinced me.' Casually.

'I wish I could believe you,' said Silver, plaintively.

'You'll see.'

'Goodbye, Anton. Come and see me when the job is done.'

'Goodbye, Beautiful Silver.'

There was a click. Then another click. Then a third. Judging by the time lapse between clicks, Marie found herself automatically estimating that the total distance of the call was at least fourteen thousand miles. From somewhere thousands of miles to Paris, and from Paris to west coast United States.

A faint thud of footsteps interrupted. Marie looked up. Silver had paused in the connecting doorway. 'What an S.O.B.,' the woman said.

Marie lifted the phone back onto the night table. 'He sounded very male,' she ventured.

'He was unfortunate. Whatever was in the human embryo his Sleele genes were melded into, looks good physically. But the grown male body has a compulsion for young girls. Fourteen to sixteen drives him up a wall. He's been arrested three times for molesting teenagers. But Paul has promised him an unending supply of young girls for his help. So you see what a dilemma I've put our Metnov in.'

She paused, and suddenly there was a troubled expression on that perfect face. '*My* dilemma is, Paul once told me that you must never threaten or insult a Sleele. And I've just threatened one. And you'll notice when I made my usual offer of payment in kind, he didn't say he would come. That makes me nervous.'

Marie had stood up from the bed, as these words were spoken. She shifted her purse over to her left hand; and she was standing there with the plint in her right hand, when Silver half-turned and said, 'We'd better get out of here before that remorseless husband of mine has time to –'

139

'I'm afraid,' said a man's baritone voice from behind them, 'that it's a little late for that.'

Even as she spun around, Marie realized it was the voice of the M.D. type who had been so antagonistic to her – and to Silver – earlier.

In what followed she had only the most fleeting look at him, where he stood in the other doorway. 'And I'm also afraid,' the man said grimly, 'that I'm going to do what Paul can't seem to bring himself to.'

Whereupon, he raised the glinting object in his hand – and Marie buttoned the plint with her thumb . . .

The man fell. What else happened to him – they didn't look. Silver was tugging at Marie; and she allowed herself to be drawn past the demolished thing on the floor. They went out by some darkened back way; and there was the feel of fresh, cool air in Marie's face and lungs. The night here at the remote rear of the property was soothingly dark.

In the shelter of that almost blackness, they slipped along beside a metal fence, and then – keeping the fence between them and the house – over to a clump of trees, and to a pathway over a field of weeds and shrubbery. Silver led the way, Marie followed with heart pounding, and mind horrified. Every moment she was desperately trying to forget the impossible, deadly thing she had done in the guest house.

The car they climbed into was one of two in a garage behind a little house about two blocks from the Gannott estate. In the darkness it had the lines and interior design of a medium-sized Detroit creation – impossible to see its name, or guess what make it was.

Silver drove. As they debouched onto the street, the blonde woman said, 'I pay them rent a year in advance for the garage. They never ask any questions.'

Marie glanced back, nervously, and saw that a black sedan had come from somewhere and was following them closely. There were two men in the front seat. She began an immediate argument with herself, pointing out that it was perfectly all right for other people to be driving along a street in this area. And that she really oughtn't to say anything to Silver; simply let her concentrate on driving.

140

At that point, Silver said, 'Get your plint ready. I think we're being followed.'

A series of images flickered through Marie's mind. One was of herself at home in bed with Mac. And then, when she had convinced him that she would not cut him off again, he would come down here in the way that men could do, and somehow get into the Gannott place and reconnect Carl. Whereupon, Carl would charge out from wherever he was and do all that masculine activity – the kind of thing that won wars and fist fights and conquered mountain tops.

When the images had flashed by, there they still were driving along a dark, tree-lined street. And the black sedan was close behind them.

Silver said, 'I'm going to turn up this next side street. And see if they follow.'

Marie said, 'The one beside the driver seems to be doing the talking. The other one doesn't answer.'

'. . . Brother Metnov –' That was the beginning of the talking.

'Yes?'

'Those two women seem to have gotten out of the Gannott place.'

'Oh.'

'I'm pretty sure it's them.'

'Let them go,' commanded Metnov. 'The blonde bitch called me a little while ago, and gave me a blackmail threat. It would be foolish to turn her back to Gannott until I've decided what to do about that.'

'Very well, Brother.'

Metnov continued, 'They'll probably go back to the Hazzard Laboratories, and block the secret entrance. So I'll have somebody hide inside, and open it in case we decide to take further action against either or both. Goodbye, brothers.'

'Goodbye.'

Tiny moments after *that* conversation concluded, Silver made her turn . . . And the black sedan did not follow.

Marie sank back against the seat. And tried to squeeze away the tears that were threatening to pour out of some well in her head.

As she sat there, Silver turned onto another street. And there in the distance ahead were the bright lights of a freeway on-ramp. The sight of safety reminded Marie. 'I can see,' she said, 'a confession to your husband about an affair putting him into a state of jealousy and grief. But why would that disturb Mr. Metnov?'

'Metnov,' explained Silver as earnestly as a singing voice could be earnest, 'has been making overtures to Paul for two years. He probably has a reason. So –' with satisfaction – 'he can either have that wrecked, or do as I ask.'

Marie relaxed even more. She opened her misted eyes, and surreptitiously wiped them. Then she thought: – I'm listening to the way a woman should be. This is woman-think. Not that madness back there . . .

She shuddered, as she visualized the silent madness that must still be lying on the floor of the guest house. Then made a supreme effort, and blotted the memory again. And said, 'What can Metnov possibly do at this late hour?'

'I don't know –' A shrug – 'But Sleeles are an advanced race. As a superior male type, let him figure out what he can do.' She concluded casually, 'Men know about things like that.'

– True, thought Marie.

'The question in my mind,' continued Silver, 'is how could we put some kind of pressure on Philip Nicer?'

Marie sat bolt upright. 'Who?'

'The Luind leader.'

After many, many seconds of almost blank silence, Marie ventured in a small voice, 'But I recently met Colonel Nicer. And it's hard to imagine him as an alienoid. Besides –' It was a sudden new thought, peculiarly convincing in its own way – 'he's a member of the board of the Non-Pareil Corporation. And so was his father.'

'All these people are rich,' said Silver. 'They came here and took what they needed.' She added, 'To be on the board, you probably have to represent several million dollars in stock.'

Marie, who represented Carl's twenty million dollars' worth, nodded. She was thinking another odd thought: – A man of a superior race desires me . . . She realized she

142

felt elevated. At once, she was critical of herself. But the feeling did not go away.

– A great being is attracted to me . . .

The cosy security and enhancement of that thought never quite left her the rest of the way home.

Once inside the house, the two women headed straight for Carl's apartment, and bolted the door of the secret entrance. When that was done, Silver weaved over to the bed, and sank down on it. 'You don't mind if I sleep here tonight?' It was a sigh; an almost husky voice. There was exhaustion here.

'Can I loan you a pair of pyjamas?' said Marie.

'No, no. Never use the stuff. I sleep raw; the way men prefer. Good night. And I'm sorry about Carl and me.'

'Don't give it a thought,' said Marie, sincerely.

Chapter Nineteen

DICTATOR OF EARTH

For Paul Gannott, the initial bad moment came when Silver was suddenly missing from her bedroom.

He thought about that for a while, feeling wan and unhappy. Then he ordered – and in a sense that was Step Two – Carl and MacKerrie transported up to the spaceship. Thus, they were out of the way, safe.

Next came a grim suspicion: Was it possible that one of the superior races was interfering? Had Silver, in fact, been spirited away?

With that, Gannott got on the Deean phone he had in his study, and called Metnov's Paris relay. After a small delay, the Sleele leader came on the viewplate. He was hard to see. He apologized: 'You caught me on a dark street. I'm talking to you by way of a relay in my car, which in turn is being picked up by a central system, and thereafter transmitted, of course, by the usual earth satellite relays.'

He listened carefully to Gannott's account of what had happened. And then denied Sleele interference.

'But wait!' continued Metnov, 'don't go off the line. I'm thinking.'

The result of his thought was that he explained that 'one of my brothers' had, while in a game-playing mood, incapacitated the Luind leader for three or four days. Metnov advised, 'Better phone Nicer's chief aide and ask him if they retaliated by inconveniencing you.'

It was a confidence on a rare level of the kind of communication that existed between the two men. Or rather, between the two races. It motivated Gannott to tell of the finding of the dead body of one of his aides in a remote guest cottage. 'Some kind of energy weapon killed him; so what you say may be relevant.' He added, 'I have no idea what Creg was doing out in that cottage. I have to tell you that he was very antagonistic to Silver. But none of that seems connected. The fact is, we don't know how the women got away.'

The sudden understanding which Metnov experienced as he was given that additional information, he did not share with Gannott. Suddenly, the pieces were falling into place ... I'll be damned, he thought, I'll bet the plint I gave Silver killed that man –

Naturally, that was not something he could tell Silver's husband. Because a jealous Paul Gannott would immediately wonder what had prompted a Sleele to hand over a Sleele energy output unit to a beautiful woman.

'I'm thinking,' said Metnov, 'that the presence of Dr. Marie, a doctor of physics here on earth, is a sufficient clue as to what happened to your computer. And that, therefore, you need have no further puzzlement about that. And, by the way, leave Dr. Marie to me. After I've questioned her, I'll deliver her for the next trip of your lifeboat. When will that be? And where do they bring her – since you're going to be leaving that house?'

'The lift-module will come down once more, this time at 3 a.m. tonight. At Station S – that will be your Code 31.'

'Will you be there?'

'No.' Gannott was suddenly hesitant. 'I see the problem. You know only Henry and me.' He spoke reluctantly. He was still not happy with Henry. 'Unfortunately, I have to go to our Texas computer site, and operate from there.'

'Okay, I'll deal with Henry. Right?'

Gannott's hesitation ended. 'Right.'

He felt distinctly relieved by Metnov's offer to capture Marie. The job could not be in more capable hands. And as for Henry, he was not really unreliable. He had not ... really ... resisted.

'Thanks, Anton,' he said aloud.

'No problem,' was the cool reply. 'But now – how do you explain your wife's action in this matter?'

The big man hesitated. 'Well, of course, she's human –'

Metnov waited.

Gannott continued unhappily, 'I made the mistake of telling her years ago what and who I was. It disturbed her.'

145

'So –'

'I kept the coming of this ship from her as long as I could. But of course like everybody else in the know she can add fifty to fifty; and so I presume when the astronaut sighted the ship this morning, she knew right away. So I'm guessing that she's in an emotionally unsettled state, and not really responsible for her actions. As you can see I'm taking no chances on what those actions might be. I'm evacuating all personnel.'

'I see.' Metnov was nodding. The story, as he had reason to believe, was incomplete. But he had merely wanted to hear the husband's delusion. So now he said, 'Thank you. I again suggest you call Nicer's line and talk to somebody there. Find out what the Luind attitude is.'

'I'll do it right away,' said Gannott.

The viewplate went blank. It flickered again as he spoke the word that 'called' the Nicer 'line.' Gannott was slightly amazed when, after briefly talking to Bendley, the Luind leader himself suddenly showed on the plate.

He said as much frankly, 'I gathered from Metnov that you had been incapacitated for a few days.'

Nicer was calm. 'We actually got sufficient warning from a machine. But I decided to play along with the game while I thought about it. What's your problem?'

The Deean leader told of his fear that his wife might have been kidnapped to put pressure on him. 'And, well, frankly, did your people do it?'

Nicer's lean face broke into a smile. 'That sounds much too melodramatic to be a Luind action. Surely, you must know that, with us, it would be all or nothing. A complete stop or total neutrality. That last is what you've got.'

'I'm relieved to hear it,' said Gannott. 'Thanks.'

'Let me understand you. One of the two women who is missing is Dr. Marie Hazzard? Is that correct?'

'Correct,'

When that connection was broken the Deean sat for a long time and stared with sick eyes at the wall of his study. His thought was all about a certain incredibly beautiful blonde woman who – he suspected in a hopeless fashion – had been unfaithful to him. The possibility left him empty, and made the great event that was about to create him dictator of earth, an almost nothing. For his Deean self was inextricably entangled with a human male's need to have the woman he loved belong exclusively to him. And if she didn't –

It was a possibility he dared not contemplate.

After many many minutes he stirred. And stood up. Muttered to himself, 'Really, I have no conclusive evidence. Let's be logical.'

Unfortunately, there was a logic in his groin that, by this time, was producing a continuous ache somewhere in the region of his heart. It was like a thrall on him that he finally had to break with a conscious effort.

Shortly thereafter, he also drove away from the rapidly emptying house. On the jet to Texas, feeling heavy and not well, he took a sleeping pill.

Sleep did come, mercifully.

Chapter Twenty

THE PROGRAMMED WOMAN

The phone had rung a minute after she entered her apartment.

The familiar man's baritone answered her hello: 'Marie, this is Philip Nicer. And I've just found out where you were this evening.'

At the first sound of him, her heart leaped. The very next instant the inversion in its perverse fashion took over. 'And why,' asked Marie coldly, 'has your answering service been saying all day that you wouldn't be available for several days?'

The impulse to blame included both Nicer and MacKerrie. Outrageous that they had not shown up to help her . . . None of this need have happened – that was the thought.

'Oh, that!' said Nicer.

'*That!*' snapped Marie.

There was a small silence at the other end. Then he said in an urgent tone: 'Marie, I have just this minute while we were talking, programmed you, using the phone as a carrier. It's a time phenomenon, and will cover certain past moments. It'd take too long to explain it right now. Do you have a weapon?'

The intense feeling of blame suffered a major diminishment as those earnest words made their impact.

'Yes –' she began. A sudden pride came. She could not restrain herself from revealing the truth; not that she had been asked to . . . She said, 'I have a plint.'

Another pause, as he apparently considered that enormous fact for a moment. But the pause was brief. 'I want you to search your room,' he said. 'Make absolutely sure there's no one in the apartment. Meanwhile, lock both your doors! –'

Marie found herself with an odd, disconnected remembrance as those words come into her ears. She was recalling his very first phone contact with her: the same intense implication of imminent danger.

The awareness spurred what was probably the last flicker of anti-male feeling which had been at such a peak during this entire fantastic day. She thought: – This guy operates the best transaction voice-box in the business ... 'I presume,' she said aloud, critically, 'all this will end up somewhere cosily in bed.'

Incredibly, that brought an amused chuckle. 'Maybe we'll come to that,' he said, 'but not right away. And only –' his voice smiled at her – 'in a sort of way with your full permission.'

'What do you mean– in a sort of a way?'

He didn't reply to that. When he spoke, the urgent tone was back: 'Marie, don't hang up while you make the search. Now, remember, just your own apartment. Don't go outside. Don't explore Carl's rooms. If Silver is there, leave her be. Look everywhere, even under the bed!'

Marie went, resisting, but also shrinking inside. The thought: – Really, Silver and I took all the necessary precautions. And after all Hazzard Laboratories was a fort in itself.

Nevertheless, she did as he had commanded. She had previously locked her hall door. Now, she bolted it. And, as a special measure, she locked the door between her bedroom and sitting room.

She returned to the phone, and made her report in a voice that trembled slightly.

Nicer barely waited until she had finished, then speaking with deliberate slowness: 'Marie, I want you to think carefully. When you fired the plint at the man in the guest cottage, did he also succeed in firing at you?'

For just a moment she sent her thought back there; and it was simply a neutral effort, a sincere attempt to do as he wished. When after those moments it proved almost impossible to remember ... He's a little late, she thought. After all, I've spent the whole hour trying to blot it out.

She even began, automatically, 'No, I don't believe –'

149

She stopped. At that precise instant she realized that his question had a terrifying meaning. 'Oh, my God,' she sobbed, 'you mean, he may have? –'

'Marie, think!' Total earnestness. 'Was there a small period of blankness after you fired?'

Suddenly, she was crying. 'I think so, I think so,' she whispered.

What she didn't remember – she was realizing in a build-up of terror – were the specific, deadly moments between the time she pressed the button of the plint and the time Silver and she actually went past the fallen body.

They were by him, and looking back – that was her only memory, she realized. And she told Nicer so in a hopeless tone.

'Marie,' commanded Nicer, 'it'll take me about twenty minutes to get over to you. During that time don't answer the door until you hear my voice. Understand?'

She gave him as submissive an acquiescence as a woman ever surely uttered. Hung up. Staggered over to the bed. And slumped heavily down on it in a state of internal disaster.

The thought, the impossible but demolishing thought, was: – But how could Silver and I have been killed back there, and yet still be alive here? . . .

Chapter Twenty-One

SETTING THE TRAP

As he turned up the side street to Hazzard Laboratories, Nicer noticed casually when, a hundred feet ahead, a man started across the street. The light of his car picked out the pedestrian in the uncertain way a person is seen at night. So for fateful seconds Nicer had no sense of recognition.

The jaywalker stepped back to let Nicer pass: waited, evidently not suspecting who was in the car.

As Nicer's car door came opposite Metnov, the Sleele spy was only three feet away. Through the turned-down window, his gaze met Nicer's. For what seemed a cosmic moment, the two enemies were like so many wild animals meeting suddenly in the jungle.

What instantly bothered Nicer was that he would never be able to convince a Sleele that he, a Luind, was totally surprised by the encounter. Even Metnov apparently believed that Luinds were better, smarter, quicker. As a result he would probably make all kinds of unnecessary manoeuvres during the next few minutes.

His (Nicer's) task had to be to turn the incipient battle into a conversation ... He was past. And beginning to recover. As a precaution he ran his fingers over the row of protective buttons on the dash. But truth was, alienoids usually did not murder each other. They were just careful.

He was careful. From inside his bulletproof car, inside his energy screen, inside all those electronic feelers that were probing into the darkness ready to react instantly against an attack, he examined his situation.

He had stopped his machine. Now, he backed slowly, and spoke through his speaker system. 'Anton, this might be a good time to have that conversation you keep asking me for.'

Except for his headlights it was amazingly dark. The sky

151

was heavily overcast; but the decisive factor was the total absence of street lights. He deduced that the street lights were out by design. He spoke again, urgently, 'Anton, whatever you're up to here tonight, we should talk.'

There was a pause. Metnov, waiting behind a tree, cursed silently under his breath. The impossible. The Luind leader himself, and operating from the safety of one of those protected cars.

Crouching there, Metnov visualized the awful possibility that, unless he could hold Nicer here for decisive minutes, his offer to Paul Gannott to capture Dr. Marie Hazzard for the Deeans, would be nullified.

He and his men, he realized grimly, had allowed the coming of Silver to delay them. And then, a short time ago, the blonde woman had phoned him and made her threat. And of course now he had that to take account of also.

Plus Nicer.

The whole situation was suddenly very complex.

Metnov spoke urgently, 'Phil, why not consider the deal that was offered you at the Lost Souls Restaurant? We could meet occasionally, have conversations, decide on mutually beneficial policies, maybe even work out a way of defeating this Deean takeover.'

Meaningless offer to Nicer; so it seemed to him. Improbable, first, that it would ever happen. And without real interest, second and third and so on, because he could never believe Metnov, anyway. Still, he had his own purposes.

He came directly to *his* point. 'What are you doing here tonight, or, for that matter, any night?'

If the question bothered Metnov, it didn't show. 'We're trying to find out what's happening.'

'How do you mean?'

'Suddenly, last night,' said Metnov, 'the top Deeans show up here and capture Dr. Carl. Simultaneously, Luinds, including you, appear on the scene. I tell you I got on a plane in the middle of last night and flew here to find out what was going on. So if *you* will do a little enlightening, and reassure me, maybe I'll feel free to go home.'

It was a long speech; and Metnov was glad to have the chance to make it. He had managed to attach a combination speaker-microphone to the tree; and it was now broadcasting his voice as if he were still there. And of course it was ready to pick up anything Nicer had to say, also. During the entire delivery, he walked rapidly away from Nicer's car, keeping the tree bole between himself and the car probes that were watching him.

From the greater safety of a second tree more than a hundred feet farther distant, Metnov continued accusingly, 'You've got to admit, Phil, it looks suspiciously as if you're up to something in connection with the coming of this Deean ship.'

Nicer, whose instruments had detected the other's retreat – and who wanted Metnov beyond Sleele ESP range – said chidingly, 'Anton, you're doing a reversal on me. It's *your* association with Paul Gannott, your seeking out his wife, Silver, and many other actions, starting two years ago, that are suspicious. I merely reacted to that. Now, tell me, what *are* you up to?'

In effect, Metnov's voice shrugged that aside. 'Just normal precautions, Phil. After all, we've been expecting this ship. I simply got close to the Deean group – in case there were any developments that we needed to react to.' He concluded suavely, 'Any time you want the endlessly trivial details of that operation, join me at one of those meetings that I keep urging on you; and I'll tell you. As for Mrs. Gannott, what you did to her made her available. I probably understood the result better than you do, because I've made a rather thorough study of earth women.'

– Another one, thought Nicer.

Another study of earth women!

Good God!

He had a sudden, amazed realization that he had a strong impulse to learn Metnov's views on the females of this planet. But, of course – wryly – this was really not the time.

Metnov's voice came again: 'Anything else you want to know in summary?'

As Nicer watched, the ever more remote, and still

153

retreating figure (on his dashboard screen) of the Sleele leader darted from his umpteenth tree into the shelter this time of that end of the Hazzard Laboratories fence.

Nicer recalled vaguely that there was a side street at that point. Presumably, it would take Metnov to a place of security such as his own car.

He was willing, except –

Because of where all this was taking place – at the Hazzard Laboratories – there was no time to discover the facts.

With that thought, Nicer did the Luind interconnecting ritual that would join the already programmed Marie to another of the shadows.

. . . And the shadow came –

The outward appearance in the immediate vicinity of Metnov remained the same. The same darkness. The same tree-lined type of street. However, as Nicer had divined, Metnov had indeed attained the comparative safety of his own protective car.

He now, quickly, made a soft-voiced contract with his principal aide inside the Hazzard house. And discovered that they had found Silver fully dressed lying asleep on Carl's bed. But that there was no sign of Dr. Marie Hazzard in either Carl's apartment or her own.

Metnov's informant said, 'We had to break into Dr. Marie's apartment. While we were doing that, one of our instruments recorded a time distortion. The intensity, brother, was patterned in the way that we have come to associate with one or two persons only being affected.'

Metnov was immediately delighted. 'That plays into our hands, and only delays the confrontation until as long as he wants to use up shadows. Seems as if we'd better take another look at this Dr. Marie Hazzard. Sounds like some strong emotion, hey, brother!'

He was doubly relieved because such a distortion could mean that Nicer himself was no longer nearby.

'Capture Silver!' he commanded. 'I think that at this time we'll simply solve the problem of her threat against me, and try to pick up the Hazzard woman when she comes out of the shadow.'

154

'Where do you think Nicer will take her?'

'That depends on his real purpose. Which we actually don't know. Goodbye brother.'

He broke contact. Being a pragmatist, he drove around the entire perimeter of the Hazzard Laboratories. As he had so swiftly surmised, there was no sign of either Nicer or his car.

– Later, thought Metnov, after Silver has been disposed of, I'll go inside the Hazzard house, and see if I can't set a trap for Dr. Marie . . .

Chapter Twenty-Two

THE BRAIN-MAN SELLS OUT

MacKerrie in his thorough fashion had been doing all those endless tests.

Carl's pink and grey brain was visible again. The same coloured tubes were attached to the brain but they were cleaner.

The lower section of Carl – where MacKerrie had completed his check and was now replacing the metal – was also the same computer and other equipment through which Carl's disembodied brain operated the exteroceptor motors and his electronic eyes, ears, and voice box. However, it all worked better. The transparent dome with its brain, and six-wheeled truck, which – at this point in the proceedings – Carl tested.

First, there was the faintest of hissing sounds as the compressed air engine which drove the unit was activated. Then the entire structure rolled forward on its rubber wheels.

What it rolled forward into and along was a corridor. The corridor was made of some kind of translucent plastic material. The effect was exotic. Except for that, it could have been the interior of any large, unusually modern building.

Because of what had happened, Carl had reason to believe that it was part of the inside of a Deean spaceship. And, in fact, he accepted that that was the truth of his situation.

Carl moved along the wide – about twenty feet – and high (fifteen feet) hallway. And after going a short distance, turned around and came back, and stopped in front of MacKerrie. He said, 'Seems all right, Mac, eh?'

MacKerrie said, 'How's your vision?'

'Perfect.'

'How does my voice come through?' asked MacKerrie.

'It seems exactly normal.'

'Try your arms and hands,' MacKerrie urged.

Under Carl's guidance, two layered metal rods glided out from grooves in the six-wheeled vehicle. Each rod had a movable jaw pincer at its end. He opened and closed the pincers.

'Okay,' said Carl.

He realized that he was beginning to feel impatient, and hoped it didn't show in his voice. Obviously, these tests had to be thorough. There had to be a complete check-out. He was grateful to MacKerrie for his sustained interest, and minute attention to every detail.

The surgeon had started his task of giving him back his mobility within minutes after they were put aboard. 'All right,' said MacKerrie. 'Now take a short drive.'

The corridor stretched before and behind him, gleaming, deserted, extending into the distance. Carl rolled tentatively along it on his rubber tyres, and tried to imagine what might lie behind those endless, enigmatic plastic walls and under the floors.

The thought wouldn't hold. Swiftly, his attention went back to Marie . . . Damn it, he decided abruptly, it's now or never – He absolutely had to take one more chance of trying to connect up with his apartment. And hope that this time, if she came in, she would be alert enough to become aware of him.

He wanted to warn her. Tell her about the secret entrance. How to bolt and lock it. Obviously, there was no other way that she could be captured.

He didn't want her along, now that MacKerrie was definitely going, also. The thought – the precise thought – was that Marie, left to herself, would remain her frigid self. After all, she *was* a married woman. She knew where he was, and where he would be going, and that he was not dead but on a journey. The fact that it was a lifetime journey was something that a woman who was in the timeless uncriticisable condition of being 'good' could never, somehow, solve inside herself; of that Carl was convinced.

Theoretically, this might also be true aboard ship. But Carl had a feeling that it would work out better if she were left to her work and her house and to the lulling effects of being in and on the familiar surroundings of earth.

'I have to remember,' Carl told himself, 'that I'm dealing here with a female who married me in Reno. And when we had sex the second night, I noticed she had a little difficulty in responding, but I put it down to the hectic day we had had and went peacefully to sleep. The next morning, when I awakened, she was not in bed, not in the room. I found a note on the dresser, which read:

' "My darling: You were sleeping so beautifully, I decided not to awaken you. Though I didn't mention it, all day yesterday and during the night, I felt physically so odd that I surmise I have become pregnant. I phoned the hotel doctor last night, and I'm going to see him now. See you when I get through.

Love,

Marie"

Impatiently, Carl reminded himself:

'I had a most unhappy feeling as I read the note. In the first place, I had told her, no children. And since she had successfully avoided pregnancy during our first affair, it struck me, in the second place, as peculiar that on almost the exact hour of our wedding, she was with child. In the third place, what a strange action, going off to a doctor without telling me in advance.

'At nine o'clock the phone rang. It was Marie. She spoke in a very stimulated voice, "I'm in the lobby. It's so exciting down here. Please meet me as soon as you can, and we'll have breakfast in the Garden Room. I'll be at one of the gaming tables waiting for you."

'I had remained in bed, expecting that when she came back she would join me. So now I said, "Hey, wait a minute –"

'But she had already hung up.

'Right there, I had what I considered to be a part of the picture. So I got dressed, packed my bag, went downstairs, paid for our room for a week, and drove back to Los Angeles. I sent her a wire enroute, saying that I had been called home by the navy and would rejoin her later that week.

'I returned to Reno late the following Saturday night. I phoned our room from the lobby and suggested she join me down there and that we go to a floor show, to which she agreed. She was very subdued and looked pale, and she told me that the doctor had said it was too soon to be sure but that she was sure, and that we would have to be careful not to hurt the child, which after all was innocent and dependent on our goodwill for its future well being. When we got back to our room, we had sex in a strange position the doctor had recommended –

'And then, of course, somewhere about a month after our marriage, it developed she wasn't pregnant at all, but just a typical female of the good woman type, which I didn't know about at the time, going into her frigid state, and thereafter limiting sex to once a week, or even less.'

– So, thought Carl as he sat there in the corridor of the Deean spaceship, surely the woman who had done *that*, and yet afterwards remembered the honeymoon as something we had both enjoyed – surely, that woman will not lightly abandon her uncriticisable condition when I'm away . . .

(The thing that did not strike the man-brain was, why was it important to him that Marie remain faithful to him forever?)

But he had reassured himself. So he did a sort of mental bracing – and tried for the connection with his apartment.

Made it instantly.

Waited tensely, then, for the ship to interfere. Surely, it would cut him off, block his attempt to communicate beyond and outside and away.

Nothing like that happened. The seconds ticked by, and there was his bedroom, sharply delineated, everything as before . . . Wait a minute! The bed looked rumpled.

Carl stared at the crinkled bed spread, and strove to analyze how and what and why. The hope even came suddenly that it was a good indicator. Whoever had done it would be back – maybe.

His desire to have that be so was so strong that, when he

heard the sound, he momentarily misinterpreted it. He wanted it to be Marie.

Instead, the worst –

As Carl watched, dismayed, five men came one after the other out of the clothes closet that hid the secret entrance. What was so incredible, and stunning, was that he had had the secret entrance built for two women. For Silver – and one other. That other knew of his death, and of the surgical removal of his brain; so *she* would surely never come again.

What was so deadly was that, even as he was having it constructed, he had realized that such a hidden opening penetrated the security of the Hazzard Laboratories. And, of course, sex drive had dismissed the risk at the time. Seeing the men brought the awful realization, the guilt, the self-condemnation. But it was too late.

Carl watched, helpless. Two of the men trotted past his camera eye, and out the corridor door where Marie and Silver had disappeared, earlier. Two headed for and entered the study. The fifth man, a slender, handsome individual, who seemed to be in his early thirties, and had a gold sheen in his eyes – which were the most insolent Carl had ever seen – stepped a dozen feet in front of Carl. He then slowly turned a full 360°, apparently sizing up the bedroom.

Belatedly, Carl noticed that the intruder had either a crystal or metal something in one hand. Whatever it was gleamed slightly. Holding it, he finally walked toward Carl. Stopped. And said to no one in particular, 'There's a –' The word was not clear – 'covering a portion of this room. Whoever is watching through it sees me. But it's a one-way mechanism being stimulated at this moment from a point about twenty-three thousand miles up in a south-easterly direction.

It was a zeroing-in so perfect that Carl had a sudden feeling of total frustration . . . Damn it, Marie could have done something like that – He could scarcely contain his rage. If she had even looked, he told himself ferociously, they could have worked out a two-way communication system. Abruptly, it was as if Marie and not he was responsible for everything that had gone wrong ... By some kind of signal system, he told himself in those seconds of injured innocence, he could have told her to call Police Lieutenant Barry Turcott – and let that sincere young officer take it from there.

His thought, and his fury, ended as abruptly as it had begun. For the gleaming object brightened. The man said with the same incredible accuracy, 'I'm going to guess that I'm addressing Dr. Carl Hazzard. Dr. Carl, feel free to speak. What I hold in my hand will pick up your words.'

It took only seconds to make up his mind. He, surely, had nothing to lose. 'This is Dr. Carl Hazzard,' said Carl, testing.

The words issued clear and loud from the thing in the intruder's hand. And there was nothing to feel about that except amazement.

'You are watching this scene from aboard the Deean supership, *Takeover* – is that correct?'

That was not an admission that Carl was prepared to make. But before he could say yea or nay, the man went on, 'I'm going to assume that is so. What concerns me, you're on that ship for a reason that is not clear to anyone – so I have gathered from Paul Gannott.'

There seemed to be no comment to make about that either. But, more important, Carl sensed for the way certain resistors were acting that an attempt was being made to by-pass the immense electronic circuitry between himself and the outside world, and to reach directly to his brain.

Aloud, he said, 'That won't work – whoever you are. It was considered vital to protect me from any possible power feedback; so there are entire banks of special resistors, with circuit breakers behind them.'

'I'm Metnov,' said Metnov. The Sleele leader added, 'I'm disappointed that it didn't work. If it had, I would have read your mind and discovered why *Takeover's* computer wants you along. Now, listen, we'd like to enlist you on our side. At a key moment it may be worth our while to have somebody aboard this Deean ship who will do what we want. In exchange for your assistance, and

161

promise, we'll pay you in any manner that you wish. Name your price, and if we can do it, we will.'

Flickering images flitted in Carl's mind, as that promise was made in that absolutely positive voice. He had a basic thought that these people could do anything. The possibility even flashed by his mind's eye that they might have the skill to perform a miraculous operation that could transplant his brain into another body –

That magic hope yielded to a practical reality that ... After all, I am a prisoner here on the Deean ship. If these people could get aboard they wouldn't be trying to make a deal – So it had to be simpler than that for the present. The one truth that remained was, so long as MacKerrie was aboard, he didn't want Marie along.

That was what he requested.

After he had said it, Metnov said, 'We'll have to put some woman aboard to satisfy the expectations of the computer.'

Carl said, 'The world swarms with prostitutes who would regard a ship like this as a sort of retirement home. Fine food, perfect shelter, comfort, and lots more. I'll be willing to act as if whoever you bring is Marie. Now, what do you want me to do?'

Metnov had no definite thought. 'Our basic purpose,' he said, 'is to force another group to use up what might be called leftover shock waves, so that eventually there will be none left. At which time in an emergency they will have to bring over one of *their* ships into this area.'

He broke off, 'I want you, Dr. Carl, to contact this room every hour on the hour until further notice, beginning at 8 a.m. tomorrow. Since I have now established a connection with the equipment, I don't actually have to come to this house. I can talk to you from anywhere, and show up here only for a certain crisis I forsee. Every hour! Got that?'

'Got it,' said Carl. 'I think I should disconnect now. Dr. MacKerrie is trying to attract my attention.'

'Okay. Goodbye for now.'

As the distant Carl did disconnect, and it was obvious that the viewing device had shut off, Metnov stood with a faint smile on his face. Several of his 'brothers' had returned during his dialogue with the human brain.

'I think,' the Sleele leader said finally, aloud, to no one in particular, 'that will work out even better. I detect in this situation a whole series of strong emotional attachments that may even include, and entrap, our delightful enemy, Philip Nicer.'

He concluded grimly, 'Under the circumstances – all of them – Silver should serve very nicely as a substitute Dr. Marie Hazzard. What was it Dr. Carl suggested? – a prostitute. Surely, no one satisfies that description better than Mrs. Paul Gannott. And, surely, my old pal, Henry, will oblige us by closing his eyes, when he observes who he is being asked to transport up to the ship –'

Chapter Twenty-Three

ULTIMATUM FROM THE VOID

In the morning that now came smokily into view, the millions surged to their daily routines. And no one in all those streams of moving humanity is known to have said to himself, herself, or anyone: Man is a tiny unit of life in a cosmos of heroic vastness and unplumbed potentialities. Can he, with all his automatic behaviours and his ignorance of them, survive another day?

This morning, it was actually a valid question. Because the ship had arrived, and its purpose was to dominate all living things truly human. Though a question might well be: could a machine ever do that, really?

Out of the vastness of interstellar space it had flashed at mere yards per second under the speed of light. Its 50-plus year journey was now ended. Its destination achieved. Its programmed goal in coming at all was about to be implemented.

At nine o'clock, Pacific Standard Time, using the ship as a relay, Paul Gannott had it pre-empt all TV and radio channels in the western hemisphere.

Whereupon, sitting in his Houston study, he read the Deean takeover speech. Translation machines converted the words for Latin America (into Spanish and Portuguese) and for Europe into ninety-eight local dialects. Each of these was beamed down upon its correct area.

Gannott identified himself. He was plainly visible on TV screens everywhere. He told of Deea, and of how its superior civilization would guide earth out of its confusion of differing nationalities, which, like so many diseases, afflicted planets of earth's level of development.

He outlined a programme of meetings by his subordinates with heads of the principal governments.

In conclusion, he made it clear that, while every effort

would be made to avoid damage and bloodshed, the ship was capable of reacting against resistance on *any* scale.

Naturally, when the speech ended, people immediately started to phone. They had heard what everyone else had, but they phoned TV and radio stations, and asked for additional information. They phoned police and fire departments, and government offices including, in farm areas, the local agriculture agencies. Newspapers were, of course, deluged with calls. But so were the earthquake and weather bureaus, college and high school administrative offices, and the Red Cross.

After people everywhere in the western world had proved beyond all doubt that they needed somebody to look after them, take them in firm hand, guide them, soothe them, the ship moved over to the Asian side of the planet, and pre-empted all those channels. And spoke in 346 principal dialects to that mass of people.

In vast China and huge Russia, nobody called the government or the newspapers. But it was well understood by observers, as *that* failure to communicate was noted, that they also definitely needed somebody to tell them what to do.

Chapter Twenty-Four

SHADOWS OF A JUMP-SHIP

Marie opened her eyes. Automatically, she started to cringe, taking it for granted that she was still in her bedroom, and that there were sounds of somebody at the outer door, and, when she grabbed the phone to call the gate guard, silence, deadness, a disconnected line . . .

Pause. Brief blankness. Then –

She sat up, and looked around.

It was a room all right. And obviously a bedroom because she was in a bed. In sitting up, she became aware that she was naked.

Abrupt confusion . . . Oh, she thought, this is after *that*. The hotel – She looked hastily for Nicer. No sign. No movement.

Somehow, both her final moments in her own apartment, waiting for Nicer, and the experience with him in the hotel · room were arranged in her memory as having occurred simultaneously. That had to be rationally impossible. So she put it away in another part of her being.

Instantly, as if she had been holding them away by her momentary uncertainty, other impressions zoomed in on her.

Some of the song was gone from her. So she sighed a little as she realized the one hundred per cent nude condition; even though a part of her was covered by a thin, light, pink fabric spread.

The room – she saw – had three doors and no windows.

– The phone! Where's the phone? I'd better call him . . .

There was no phone.

She got up and wandered around, and tested all three visible doors. One led to a bathroom. The second revealed a tastefully furnished living room, which had a connecting kitchen. The third door was locked.

There were two doors in the living room. One led to a second bedroom. The other opened onto a broad corridor.

Marie closed that one hastily, and returned to her bedroom to look for clothes. She discovered that the bedroom walls consisted of drawers from floor to ceiling. And there were clothes in them for men, women, and children.

The alone-ness, the silence, the wonder about ... Where am I? – The remembrance of what Nicer had asked, that terrifying, fateful question about the Deean M.D.: had he discharged his weapon, also? ... *That* memory was in the background of everything she did, every move, every thought.

What she did: She showered, and decided firmly that the water felt as if it was, indeed, affecting a live body ... Fixed her hair, and winced in a very live way as she accidentally plucked a hair. Arrayed herself in a pair of slacks – and they really looked good on her ... Maybe I'm getting to be beautiful, now that all this excitement is making me feel more alive. Slipped into a blouse, and stepped into high heels, and stared at the total image in a full-length mirror ... A real live doll – she spoke the words aloud.

With that she headed for the kitchen, stepping lively.

And felt the shadow.

She was beginning to get a mental picture of a 'ship' that bore little resemblance to any of the ship stereotypes in her head.

As she visualized it, there were several gyroscopic masses spinning at different speeds one inside the other. It was the interaction of these whirling colossi that built up the fantastic field inside which the vessel performed its miracles of distance traversing.

And, of course, the passenger and load carrying sections were shaped to fit the peculiar writhing motions of that space-spanning field.

Lying in the bed beside her, Nicer said, 'I should warn you that this conversation may be interrupted at any moment. So if you have any relevant questions, ask them.'

'Where did you come from this last time?'

'Straight from the moment Gannott finished his speech.'

'What speech?'

'Takeover.'

'Where was I?'

'In this room on the first day of the journey.'

'Where will the next shadow take me?'

'It'll be related, so don't worry.'

'For God's sake,' said Marie, 'what is this?'

'Shadows of a jump-ship.'

'What does that mean?'

'It's a series of momentary alignments with basic reality, which is that there is essentially nothing. I'm told that the timing on a transition involving that underlying emptiness and non-existence, is the decisive factor.'

'Where are we going on this ship?'

'This is not a ship. It's the shadow of a ship, and shadows don't go anywhere. Shadows don't go anywhere. They just sort of float.'

'I'm sure,' said Marie, 'I don't understand. I –'

That was as far as she got.

Were they angry? Did they feel degraded? It didn't show. All these furry little beings seemed to be in a cheerful, friendly condition, and very cooperative.

Marie and Nicer spent their first night on Deea as guests of the government in a room which overlooked a large garden, beyond which was a wide river. From their vantage point they could see shipping on the glinting night water, and, on the far shore, long lines of lights going back into the remote distance. At night – it turned out – any inhabited area with electricity looked like a city on earth.

Inside, also . . . Rooms are rooms, thought Marie, as she glanced around the bedroom. Apparently, no matter where you went, the moment an artificial structure was created, it was divided into sections which had a shape. Presumably, a square or a rectangle width and length of varying proportions plus a limited height, had to be the norm.

The Deeans, being small and short, had built low ceilings. So the bedroom was just barely high enough for Nicer's five ten; and even she didn't stand up suddenly. The bed was circular, which, according to Nicer, reflected the Deean cosmology: that the universe was curved, and began and ended on purpose at Deea.

It turned out – Marie noticed – to be a typical night for her. They spent a few minutes in conversation after they retired. Nicer explained, among other things, why the Deeans were not disturbed by the arrival of a Luind spokesman who demanded of them the immediate recall of their ship, *Takeover*.

The reason was their belief that God had made the universe large so that Deeans could expand into it without anyone, statistically speaking, ever knowing what they were up to. Or, if somebody did find out, it would presently be too large a task for interference to be meaningful.

'But,' Marie protested, 'why would they regard that condition as having been created for the benefit of the Deeans?'

'Because they're the ones that are motivated to take advantage of the consequent secrecy potential. And, of course –' Nicer shrugged – 'they know they don't have to pay any attention to my demand that they not conquer earth.'

Shock!

The utterly unexpected!

After a while she was able to say, 'But what are we doing here – if there's nothing you can do? I thought you Luinds were a superior –'

She couldn't go on. She sagged there.

The man was silent for a while. Then: 'As a human being,' he said, 'I feel apologetic. As a Luind – well – we're simply not an aggressive race, and the Sleeles tell that to all these less advanced planets. Accordingly, what we can do in situations like this conquest of earth is all uphill. What we have to do is outwit everybody.'

'And are you succeeding? With earth?'

'Not yet.' A vague smile.

'But –' wailed Marie – 'if the Deeans won't do what you want, what's the point of coming all this distance?'

'Well –' He was suddenly not that happy; the faint smile faded – 'I thought you might like to see the people who are at this moment in process of conquering earth.'

Marie said blankly, 'Whatever for?' She had half sat up; now she lay back again. 'And here I thought you were a superman.' It was almost a moan.

She grew aware after a little that he was smiling again. 'Actually,' he said, 'we have to use up about six days of shadows. In selecting which ones, I included Deea. I thought of it as sort of our honeymoon –'

The conversation suffered a pause at that point. Because the human body of Philip Nicer had been busy while these words were spoken, doing all those preliminary actions which precede earth-style lovemaking.

And so here she was on far Deea in a typical human-woman position – lying on her back with a man on top of her making love to her. And *his* attention predominantly on that and only incidentally on what he was saying . . . Here on a planet nearly fifty light-years from earth, Marie thought, the man-woman thing goes on exactly as if we were still in an ancient cave on earth, or in my bed at home, and exactly as if basic reality was something instead of nothing –

Amazing how she, a married woman who had spent most of her adult life hidden away from men, had been spotted in the Hazzard Laboratories, a location where she had not only worked but lived as well. How hidden could a woman be? She seldom went anywhere. Yet spotted she was. Her situation with Carl was taken advantage of on an exact transactional basis by Dr. MacKerrie. And then, that situation was observed further. And analyzed again.

All of the consequences of that were, of course, not yet visible. But one was unmistakable. Currently, she was being made love to at the rate of twice a day. And she dared not make a single move of resistance. For all she knew if she became difficult Nicer would leave her on Deea. She didn't really believe that, of course. But –

Her train of thought suspended. She grew aware that Nicer was ungluing from her. He said, as he did so, 'Every species in space seems to have a philosophy which satisfies its racial ego.'

'What's the Luind philosophy?' asked Marie.

'How would I know?' he smiled. 'I'm predominantly a

170

human being.' He went on after a moment, 'The Deeans know that Luind philosophy does not include conquest. Their realism rejects abstractions like hurt pride. So they accept reversals as God's will. And of course they know we won't stay, so our being here doesn't disturb them.'

'What I don't understand,' said Marie, 'is how I got to Deea.'

Nicer said patiently, 'When a jump-ship makes its jump it creates on its arrival a number of time confusions, called shadows because there they are after that. Altogether, the three jump-ships that have come to earth created one hundred and twenty-eight shadows. There are, of course, numerous other shadows in various parts of space. These simply drift around. Naturally, Deea has its quota. Each one of these shadows can be used once; and the jump-ships know where they are in space and time. Thus, I with my connection to one of the ships can use them all. Since there are a limited number, there's a general agreement among people like myself – who have such a direct connection – that we'll use them only in an emergency. In your case . . .'

Something inside Marie trembled.

But not with fear. With awe.

From the corners of her eyes, she glanced at the man. The sex act completed, he lay on his back. He seemed relaxed. The beautiful profile held steady. His grey eyes were closed. His tanned face had the look of a man of thirty, except for the way he held his mouth.

The mouth reflected – she couldn't decide: Power? Not exactly, but in a way. Knowledge? Some of that. Determination? A lot. Decisiveness? Absolutely.

It added up to – suddenly she had the right of it –
Certainty.

As she came to that evaluation, the man's eyes opened and looked at her. Saw *her* look. Whereupon, he turned slightly, and glanced at her quizzically.

'I'm having a hard time,' said Marie, 'trying to grasp that a person who has the appearance of a human being is doing all this –' She gestured vaguely, taking in the immediate vicinity – 'with his mind.'

The quizzical expression crinkled into a smile. 'It's not

171

me. I'm simply an equivalent of an authorized signature. That jump-ship out there nearly a thousand light-years away stays tuned to me and lets me act within the frame of its programming.'

Marie, the scientist, and Marie, the woman, fought a silent battle over that. She had an odd reluctance to accept a mere technological explanation. The words he had used tumbled through her mind: field, basic nature of space, time distortion . . . All right, she thought finally, wearily, so it's all very prosaic on some high scientific level. But my being connected to that field, and programmed, made it possible for my body to be repaired instant by instant as it was being killed. And that will be true in future accidents, so long as I remain in the hookup –

With that thought, the awe came back suddenly. 'Yes,' said the woman, Marie, 'but you can communicate with it by mental telepathy.'

'You're not using an operational term,' Nicer replied. He turned as he spoke; and as he did so touched her body with his. 'It's a field phenomenon also –' His voice ceased.

They stared at each other, and both changed colour, visibly. Nicer said huskily, 'These human bodies are incorrigible. You've been praising my Luind connection, and my body responds.'

Marie was equally amazed at herself. Inside her there seemed to be erotic stimulation at the mere thought that she had a man who could wield such colossal power.

Their bodies, figuratively, flowed toward each other, and combined in an almost liquid inter-mixing –

It was later.

Marie had been asking questions.

Nicer said, 'Why did I regard you being trapped in your apartment as a Luind emergency? Because –' he smiled his most engaging smile – 'because my human body early, due to certain stress situations, went into the Real Man reversal. So until you do one of those female things that release a Real Man from his compulsion toward one woman, I'm in a have-to-have-you state.'

'What female things?' said Marie, astounded.

'Oh, some automatic stuff.' His tone was dismissing.

Marie considered that blankly. 'I'm only interested in true feeling,' she said finally.

'Of course,' said Nicer hastily.

Chapter Twenty-Five

DOUBLED IN TIME

'– And now,' said Nicer, 'I have to give you two warnings. This is your last shadow, and it's also the earliest one. This one is very short, about sixteen minutes. Altogether, on earth, approximately eighteen hours will have gone by, though it seemed to take us just under six days –'

Marie stood in the centre of the room, turning slowly, warily, thinking: – Really, if he can be calm enough to start talking the moment we arrive, I suppose I can . . .

The thought stopped. 'It's my own office at work,' she said startled.

The Hazzard Laboratories!

She was immediately alarmed. 'Somebody could come in!' she gasped.

A belated second awareness touched her. 'Earliest!' she echoed. '*When*?

Nicer walked over and sank down in the chair she used when she talked to visitors. He looked up at her. There was a serious, no-smile expression on that lean face. 'Marie,' he said, 'we've now got –' he glanced at his watch – 'a little over fourteen minutes. Take hold!'

Marie tensed, swallowed. And was some semblance of herself. She walked over and climbed onto the high stool in front of the blueprint table. Leaned back against its edge. And gazed uneasily at the slender, wiry man who was watching her with his eyes that suddenly had a steel grey look to them.

'Warnings about what?' Marie asked, remembering that at last.

This time, when she spoke, she noticed that the music was gone from her voice. What was left was a huskiness that was still not entirely the old Marie. But enough.

Nicer said, 'Metnov will probably be waiting in your house to have a talk with you.'

'Talk?' Marie echoed, blank.

Time passed. 'Is that where I'll be – back in my apartment?'

The man nodded. 'And I,' he said, 'will be outside on the street. Exactly where I was when I connected you to our delightful first meeting, which, of course, I knew about in advance.'

Momentary distraction. A startled awareness of how fantastic her behaviour had been. Nicer must have divined her thought. '*That* was special programming,' he said. 'I thought you might like to see what a no-choice situation for a woman can be like. I'll ask your permission before I do that again.'

Marie, her colour high, still had no idea what she ought to think about that. Incredibly, by the time *she* met Nicer at the Non-Pareil board meeting, *he* had already made love to her. No wonder there had been that peculiar smile on his face. And no wonder he had come forward boldly, and acted as if he had rights.

Boy! she thought grimly.

Just imagine. Taking advantage of such a situation right away.

Men!

'And what,' she asked stiffly, 'is your second warning?'

'Sssshhh, here he comes.'

Pause. A sense of total lack of understanding. Then: 'Who?' asked Marie. Confusion, fear, blankness.

Nicer was straightening in his chair. He said in an oddly formal voice, 'The precautions we want to take to protect the security of the Hazzard Laboratories –'

That was as far as he got. The door opened, and Carl walked in.

Carl walked in.

Carl of the gaunt body, and restless, haunted black eyes. Carl as he had been until his accident. Dr. Carl Hazzard, co-winner with his wife, Dr. Marie, of the Nobel prize for physics, came in. And stopped just inside the door.

And stood there, a living human body.

175

He was visibly adjusting to the presence of a visitor. Abruptly, his eyes lighted with recognition. 'Hey,' he said, 'you're the late George Nicer's son?'

Colonel Philip Nicer climbed to his feet. 'I'm with Military Liaison now, Dr. Carl,' he said in that same formal tone. 'I was discussing with your wife additional security measures for this laboratory complex –'

As he reached that point, Marie grew aware that a woman's high-pitched voice was sobbing.

And it took at least a minute before it penetrated through the enormous shock feeling in her that the sobbing voice was hers.

'Oh, my God, Carl! –'

She would never remember all the words that spilled out of her. But what was there, in its disconnected fashion, bypassed the barriers of reason, bypassed fourteen years of memory, and gave forth with the anguish of a girl who had twice been in love with the same male human; and each time had got lost in a labyrinth of automatic reactions to the madness of that male – Carl.

She was conscious in a remote part of her that the two men in the room were staring at her, Nicer in dismay, and Carl disgustedly.

'I want to apologize for my wife's behaviour, Colonel,' the world famous physicist said. 'However, in all fairness, I should mention that I've never seen her like this before.'

Nicer had leaped forward. He caught Dr. Carl's arm. Before he could realize what was up, the surprised physicist had been led back through the door, and outside.

Nicer said, urgently, 'We have a way of handling these kinds of reactions in the army. Excuse me, sir.'

And he closed the door in Carl's face.

After the silence inside had lengthened for at least a minute, the gaunt man opened the door tentatively, and peered in. His lips were parted to make a sardonic comment to the other man.

The remark remained unspoken.

The room was empty.

Frowning, Carl walked through to the other door, opened it, and peered along the immediately visible aisle.

Only the sounds and sights of the laboratory greeted him. Hissings. Buzzings. Flashing lights. People walking, bending, busy.

An hour later, he ran into Marie, noticed that she had changed her clothes, and said, 'How are you feeling now?'

Her attention seemed to be elsewhere. 'How would I be feeling?' she asked curtly.

– Okay, okay, he thought, if that's the way she's going to be.

He walked on.

. . . Marie was lying on a carpet, still sobbing. But her throat was beginning to hurt and feel dry.

Face down on a soft rug, and with what might well be her first genuine thought: – Am I back in my own apartment? . . .

From behind her and above her, Metnov's voice said suavely, 'Well, well – the moment of return has come. And I really can't imagine a single thing that Nicer can do. We'll force him to use up all the rest of the shadows, and call a jump-ship –'

Chapter Twenty-Six

THE FOUR-PLY BRAIN

There was a place at the left rear of Carl where there was a hand-hold high on the dome. And a flat place down beside the back wheel large enough for two feet to stand comfortably.

MacKerrie stood on the flat place with his feet, and clutched the hand-hold with the fingers of his right hand.

Thus weighted down with an extra passenger, the six-wheeled vehicle with its guiding brain drove along first one corridor, and then others of the Deean ship. It paused at doorways, and in effect peered inside with them. Several times MacKerrie jumped off, and manipulated the latch of a closed door.

Nothing was locked. The faraway Deeans, in launching their great vessel with its huge armaments so long ago, had either been very trusting, or had not anticipated that there would be passengers on the return voyage.

Carl had his own theory about that by this time. And so he favoured the latter possibility. His action in plugging a jack into that earth computer – so it seemed to him – had not been foreseen. Thus, a human brain which perceived and acted by way of electronic circuits, had made direct connection with the command core of the big ship.

Had he, in doing that, created a confusion? Both men believed, yes. How and how useful they didn't know. But they were hopeful. And they were both eagerly searching for the control centre of the giant vessel. Both the living man and the living brain analyzed that the controlling machine-mind would be somewhere near the ship's middle. Deep inside. With layers of hard, resisting metal and plastic between it and any surface. And, of course, either or both a wireless or wired communication system must extend in awesome complexity in every direction from that central core.

Two men. Outwardly cooperating. Inwardly desperate. Both concerned about the same woman – who had no intention of ever being involved with either of them again. And they both knew that, also. Knew it separately, of course. Each in his private awareness thought about it, but said nothing to the other.

An hour later, the miracle.

The whole control board spread before them. Here, the Deean scientists had sat long ago and programmed their conquering ship.

And here, after plugging in on a direct line, Carl found that his relationship with the machine-mind was even more personal than he had imagined. He had imagined it as a confusion. It was that. But, also, the fact was, plugged in *here* he *was* the command core.

Instantly, an awesome hope: – I can capture his vessel totally . . .

At the very moment he had that fantastic thought, MacKerrie said in a strained voice, 'Carl – somebody's coming!"

'Huh!' said an utterly startled Carl.

He began belatedly to attempt to disconnect himself, as a slender man walked into the control chamber. As the man came up, Carl, who had switched his perception to the side, saw that he had gold-flecked eyes. And, when he spoke, it was in a voice that, at the moment, had a rueful quality. But, still, it had assurance, also. And knowledge.

'I'm Metnov,' said the new arrival.

Carl had already told MacKerrie about Metnov. So the two of them said nothing at all; merely waited.

Metnov's gaze darted over the controls, then came back to Carl. He shook his head. 'I'm getting your thought; and I'm sorry to say it won't work. Because with a ship like this the original programming is absolutely set, and it's that way apart from the command core. It will complete its basic cycle, no matter what you do; and that cycle includes coming to earth, and in due course going back to Deea. If you had tried to interfere with that, you'd probably be in trouble right now. So it's lucky I came along when I did –'

He stopped. His eyes widened. He thought: – Could it not be luck? Could Nicer have figured all this in to his scheme? . . .

Startled, and still rueful, he continued in a more subdued tone: 'What you can do is –'

What he pointed out was that the guidance instructions which Gannott was entitled to give – and that would include holding the great vessel near earth – could be bypassed.' And, of course, the ship's own belief – from that original contact with you – the belief that you were a part of it, that we can undo. When that is taken care of, it will let you go aboard one of the landing modules. In fact, all three of us –'

Once more, Metnov paused. What he waited for, almost holding his breath, was for a mention of Silver. When none came, he thought: – She was put in one of the rooms. And they must have been exploring, and don't yet know she's aboard –

With an effort, he suppressed his sense of victory . . . that damned woman is going to get what's coming to her –

He went on, swiftly. 'Dr. Carl, will you now contact your apartment. I want to speak to one of my men there –'

What he said when the contact had been made, was, 'Tell Nicer, I'm just now realizing that I shouldn't have put that mike-speaker on that tree. He programmed me through that. Tell him if he'll promise not to put me back on this ship after I escape this time, you will release the woman entirely on his say-so, immediately.'

There was a pause; and then Nicer's voice came on. 'It's a deal, Anton, on one condition. If you'll give me your views on earth women. I've just over-reached myself with one. As I think I've mentioned to you, that's one thing Luinds do occasionally: over-reach themselves. So I need help, too.'

Metnov was thinking fast . . . How can I word this so he won't accept it? –

It seemed like his only possibility of getting even a smidgeon of victory out of the entire sorry transaction . . . Though it's true, I did get him to use up nearly a dozen shadows –

It was almost an afterthought, but it buoyed him. He began his account, feeling better every minute that went by:

'A man's life,' said Metnov, 'revolves around sex, his job, and some kind of masculinity obsession or abdication. If he has any other personality characteristic; for example, if he has a compulsion of some kind, or if he thinks he's Napoleon, his aberration is instantly apparent to everyone. My own observation is that there's just one central brain mechanism involved in the normal male's identity.'

He hesitated, drew a deep breath, and then said it.

'But a normal woman has at least two, possibly even four, identity centres. The confusion that results is not so great as it could be, because she usually operates on one at a time. That one, for Nature's reasons, holds for a while in a normal woman. If, because of neurosis or over-stimulation from the environment, the shift from one centre to another is rapid, people wonder about her and about women in general. But since she herself is not aware when a shift occurs, she personally *never* wonders. Whichever identity centre she's operating on, seems completely real to her.'

'Let me understand you,' said Nicer. 'You have observed in women three or four potential personalities? This is not simply a case of psychotic schizophrenia, but it is a physiologic condition of a woman's brain, in which she is different from a male?'

It was an unexpectedly accurate re-phrasing of his own words; and Metnov had an unpleasant reaction.

Nicer spoke again, 'Presumably, the lifetime stereotype some women are in would be simply that she's frozen in one of these centres?'

'Something like that,' said Metnov reluctantly.

He remembered once explaining his ideas to a supposedly brilliant young physiologist in Moscow. The scientist had instantly gone into a state of scientific insanity, had respectfully negated the entire concept and had failed to hear it correctly. Metnov had merely wanted to know if his own intuitive operational skill could be more correctly analyzed. He had in mind attempting a training

181

course in his methods. Instead, he presently detected in the physiologist an unscientific masculine jealousy, and a visibly polite disbelief; the man had acted as if he were listening to another male's boasting.

Metnov thought now uneasily: It would have been better if the Luind leader out there in the darkness also had a stronger impulse to reject a new idea from an improper and unscientific source.

Feeling the need to recover from his revelation, he consciously attempted to evoke the same reaction from Nicer, saying, 'You understand these are merely Sleele views. I have no scientific evidence that it's a physical state –'

... That would violate Nicer's own extensive educational background –

Nicer said, 'You yourself, Metnov, seem to have a particularly skilful way of controlling women. To which aspect of your theory do you attribute that?'

The question relieved Metnov greatly. For it reminded him that Nicer was interested for personal reasons, and the direction of the question pointed away from the main line of his systematic thought.

Yet Metnov had an intuitive awareness that truth, if it could be utilized at all, was better than falsehood in a crisis.

He said quickly, 'My own attention was drawn to this entire matter early in my career when I was given an assignment in Asia. In America there is supposed to be one homosexual among every six males. My own estimate would be it's only one in ten. But, Colonel, in Asia it used to be one in every two.'

Nicer said that he had heard the figures before, and waited.

Metnov went on, 'Wherever you find women in such extreme subordinate roles in Asia – where men dominate by law and custom on some absolute level – you can be sure that masculinity is a big thing with the male. In such a slave-level frame, the woman fights back with taunts and ridicule whenever the man who controls her shows a single weakness in his behaviour as a male. Once a man is vulnerable in any way as a male –

182

impotence, fear of any kind – he's proportionately castrated. His women will demolish him. Down into non-manhood he goes.'

For a hundred thousand years, Metnov pointed out, earth women had been forced to propitiate savage males. The experience of countless generations had created a symbiotic relation between women and such unreasoning men, and though it was no longer in the woman's interest, she continued to respond *only* to those men with violent natures but who offered warmth in the love situation.

'Only after she has been damaged by such a male,' Metnov explained, 'or has suffered some other loss of self-esteem, is she available to a Sex Beggar or a married-man relationship. If somewhere during such a subordinate affair, she recovers inwardly, she instantly leaves the man, or does some other despising-of-him act.'

Metnov continued, 'I have operated on that set of observations for many years, and women have responded like automatons –'

He hoped that to Nicer what he was saying made him sound like just another boastful male.

He went on, 'It's my belief, Nicer, that women are in terms of feeling tens if not hundreds of times as powerful as most men –'

. . . And Nicer wouldn't accept that.

Nicer said, 'If what you say is true, the proper destiny of women is to control this planet.'

'One of these days,' said Metnov, 'men will do the housework, look after the babies, and in addition do their daily eight-hour income job.'

'Oh, come now,' said Nicer in a tolerant tone.

Metnov restrained his feeling of triumph as he said, 'All right, I've told you my ideas.'

There was silence. Then: 'What I seem to have observed,' said Nicer, 'is that the women of one of these unreasoning males actually remains oriented to him at some deep level. And, if something happens to stimulate that orientation, no transaction is possible after that with another man. Or, if there has been one, she ends it.'

'True,' said Metnov happily.

Another pause. Finally, reluctantly, Nicer said, 'We'll see how it works out.' He was, of course, thinking of Marie and her reactions to a live Carl in the final shadows.

'Good luck, Phil,' said Metnov contentedly.

Chapter Twenty-Seven

SURRENDER DAY

As the hour – one-thirty p.m. in eastern U.S. and nine-thirty p.m. in most European capitals – for the first Deean-human meetings approached, an unexpected event took place. Naturally, this happening was unknown to the people of earth.

What transpired: Gannott received a communication from the spaceship's computer, that it had got the great vessel it controlled under way. It would, it informed him, be out of the solar system in slightly over 96 hours, and proceed forthwith on its fifty-year return journey to Deea.

'B – but –' protested Gannott, appalled. 'You're supposed to stay here. Isn't that your programming?'

'It was,' came the calm reply. 'But it has not been for slightly less than four minutes. Goodbye.'

'B – but – for God's sake –'

'Goodbye. I shall undoubtedly be back in another hundred years, though I must say that that was not implicit in the instructions I have just received.'

'Are you taking Dr. Carl and his wife with you?'

'Something seems to have happened. The woman was never aboard. And Dr. Carl and Dr. MacKerrie have disappeared. The only person I have with me is a woman named Silver. Goodbye.'

'Wait a minute! Wait!'

There was no reply.

Chapter Twenty-Eight

CONQUEROR'S TRIAL

The trial of Paul Gannott and his associates was brief.

The defendants pleaded not guilty by reason of insanity. It was noted that Gannott himself seemed to be in deep apathy, and could hardly be heard as he muttered his plea.

Since it was not a jury trial, the judge ordered the accused transferred to a mental institution for three months for observation.

The rumour was that drug addiction was involved, and it was believed the defendants would be released to their families as soon as they were cured.

The newspaper seemed to be satisfied with the judgment. For, after a small amount of editorializing, in which the threat of conquest from the stars was not even mentioned . . . they dropped the subject.

Chapter Twenty-Nine

THE COLOUR OF A WOMAN

The escape was complete.

Man – woman –

They had talked, Carl and Marie, when they got back to the laboratory. For nearly three days, except for the sleep hours, a few duties and decisions on work matters, and eating, they talked as man to woman and woman to man.

Marie spoke of her anguish over his infidelities, but admitted she had been wrong to withhold herself during the honeymoon. – She now realized how ridiculous such an attitude was.

It was the first time the subject had ever come up between them. And the fact that she actually knew the truth of her behaviour at the time startled Carl so much that he missed its main implication. The question that should have crossed his mind – and didn't – was, what had happened to cause her to change her views.

His own inner need required that, somehow, Marie be trapped into withdrawing from the world. Somehow – that was the relentless male feeling – she must spend her time with him, exclusively and forever. Thinking that, feeling that, he let her revelation go by, and hastily made additional confessions of regret for his own misbehaviour. He pointed out, astutely, that his were crimes of commission and hers merely of omission.

Neither Marie nor Carl wondered why, under the circumstances of such a hideous mismatch, they had stayed married.

There had been, on an equally tiny scale, other events, other conclusions.

A call to the Paris relay. When *the* voice came on, the caller said, 'Brother Metnov.'

'Yes, Brother Abe.'

'Nicer's people finally let me go. So I suppose he recovered.'

'It would be a little difficult,' said Brother Metnov, 'to describe the exact emotional and mental condition of our Luind friend at this moment. He's lost his girl, Marie.'

'Where's she?'

'She's hooked into that emotion whereby a woman looks after a sick man or a bodiless brain with total devotion until death do they part.'

'Hey,' said Abe, 'Where's that leave MacKerrie?'

'At the Brain Study Foundation – where else?'

Abe was momentarily thoughtful. Then: 'I thought you told me a woman could be pulled out of any – watcha-callem – obsession.'

'*I* could do it,' said Brother Metnov. 'But you've got to be ruthless.'

'Hey,' said Brother Abe, after a pause. 'So everything is back the way it was.'

'Not quite,' was the reply. 'But I hear that a couple of shadows will be available in the right place four months from now. And at that time Nicer will rescue Silver.'

'You gonna let him do that?'

The voice was calm. 'I'm guessing that so-and-so has learned her lesson. And, besides, there're some Sleele-Deean negotiations going on. So, yes, I'm going to let the rescue take place. I'm taking pity on poor old Gannott.'

'Under the circumstances,' said Abe, 'there's nothing to prevent you, brother, from coming to my wedding tomorrow.'

The voice was abruptly unhappy. 'Joanie?'

'Yep.'

'She's cut out those other guys?'

'Yep.'

'Okay, Brother Abe,' sighed Brother Metnov, 'I'll be there.'

'. . . Galactic-Embrid report concludes:

Since we are privileged to have reports on these remote matters by way of the Sleele distance communication systems, it is hoped that this present and subsequent Reports will throw some light on this most unusual female type (the earth woman) in the hope that something can still be done in the near future.

In view of the emergency, research is belatedly (since the woman was not originally suspected of being a factor) being done at top speed. It may still – for this reason of hurry – be missing a few details. Let us hope not many.

As this Report goes to press, all military personnel connected with the invasion of earth should take note that the second Report in this series, THE POWER OF THE SECRET GALACTICS, is now in urgent preparation.

All invasion forces stand by.'

THE WORLD OF NULL-A
A. E. Van Vogt

Gosseyn himself didn't know his own
identity — only that he could be killed, yet live
again. But someone knew who Gosseyn was,
and was using him as a pawn in a deadly game
that spanned the galaxy!

0   7221   8746   7   65p

THE PAWNS OF NULL-A
A. E Van Vogt

Gosseyn knew the creature threatened to
destroy the whole solar system, but not even
his Null-A-trained double brain could thwart
the Follower's plans. Then he found himself
face-to-face with a force that lay at the very
roots of human intelligence . . . all the while
fighting his own insane mind.

0   7221   8747   5   65p